TROLLHUNTERS
TALES OF ARCADIA
FROM GUILLERMO DEL TORO

ANGOR REBORN

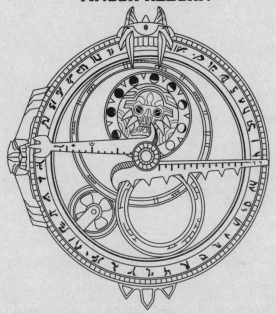

Written by Richard Ashley Hamilton
Based on characters from DreamWorks Tales of Arcadia series

Simon Spotlight
New York · London Toronto Sydney New Delhi

SIMON SPOTLIGHT
An imprint of Simon & Schuster Children's Publishing Division
1230 Avenue of the Americas, New York, New York 10020
This Simon Spotlight paperback edition December 2018
DreamWorks Trollhunters © 2018 DreamWorks Animation LLC. All Rights Reserved. All rights reserved, including the right of reproduction in whole or in part in any form. SIMON SPOTLIGHT and colophon are registered trademarks of Simon & Schuster, Inc. For information about special discounts for bulk purchases, please contact Simon & Schuster Special Sales at 1-866-506-1949 or business@simonandschuster.com.
Designed by Nick Sciacca
Manufactured in the United States of America 1018 OFF
10 9 8 7 6 5 4 3 2 1
ISBN 978-1-5344-2862-1 (hc)
ISBN 978-1-5344-2861-4 (pbk)
ISBN 978-1-5344-2863-8 (eBook)

THE MEANTIME

Angor Rot had nothing left to give.

He'd traded two fine mules at the port of Alexandria for directions to her last known whereabouts. At first the Egyptian sailors had been hesitant to do business with a Troll. But Angor Rot's desperation—plus his offer to throw in the second mule—convinced them to divulge the location.

Next to go were his goats, which Angor Rot bartered away at Cyprus. During previous travels to the island, he'd been captivated by its white sand beaches and towering Mount Olympus. This time, though, the Troll visited with an urgency in his soul. He haggled with a blind woman for what felt like hours, causing the Troll's anger to rise. Despite his name, Angor Rot had been legendary among his tribe for his calm, even temper. But this old crone sorely tested his patience before she'd revealed the incantation he'd need for the summoning.

Finally, after weeks of grueling travel across the stormy Aegean Sea, Angor Rot sold the rest of his animals at a night bazaar in Istanbul. Just as his village had been destroyed—another casualty of Gunmar the Black's conquest of the Troll world— so, too, did Angor Rot know he must also say good-bye to his beloved menagerie. Such was the cost of access to the Black Sea beyond Istanbul . . . and the sorceress Angor Rot sought.

As his lone oar dipped into its still waters, Angor Rot considered what was left of his raft. It had once been a mighty Troll vessel—an ark he captained across moonlit oceans to explore the surface lands and add their diverse animals to his growing herd. With its Graven Garb sails and crystal masts, the ship outraced pods of Kelpestrum and withstood typhoons. But now, Angor Rot stood on flotsam, on timbers held together with little more than rope and rage. He looked up at the enormous moon above him. He never felt so small, so powerless, so alone.

Alone, that was, save for his last dove. Angor

Rot had found the bird injured on the Barbary Coast after a passing squall. With his delicate stone fingers, he nursed the scrawny, deplumed thing back to health. The Troll watched him grow into a beautiful dove with a dark circlet of feathers around its neck. He may have been able to part with the other birds in his flock, but not *this* bird.

The raft scraped against the desolate coast of Bulgaria, and Angor Rot prayed that his long quest was at an end. By the light of his torch, he sidestepped evidence of past shipwrecks and saw the entrance to the cave. It appeared exactly as described by the Egyptian sailors, imposingly dark and forbidden. Angor Rot's yellow eyes searched the shadows.

"Bu rah naazga," said Angor Rot in the way the blind woman taught him. *"K'eh hazu."*

He waited for a response, the torch's glow flickering across his pockmarked body. Angor Rot's very soul shone through the wounds he'd acquired during one of Gunmar's raids. But the inner light dimmed along with his hope when no answer came. Then, the terrible knowledge of what Angor Rot must do next came to him. He had traded his every worldly possession to find this place.

3

Why should now be any different? thought Angor Rot, his heart sinking.

The Troll removed his prized dove from the nest in his belt pouch. On mended wings, the bird flew into the cave. Angor Rot heard him coo for the final time, followed by what sounded like the sickening snap of a twig. Something then moved inside the cave, shadows shifting against shadows. Finding his voice again, Angor Rot said, "I call you forth. Argante."

That's what they called her on the North Sea, where he traded his sails for animal feed.

"Pale Lady."

Another name he heard whispered in the mountain regions, where he sold the crystal masts.

"Baba Yaga."

The name they used for her in the Black Forest, where he surrendered his shepherd staff.

"Eldritch Queen," he said, remembering the name from the bedtime fables Troll parents told to frighten their misbehaving younglings.

Morgana, Angor Rot thought finally.

No one ever dared to call the sorceress by her true name. For even though she had long since disappeared after the Battle of Killahead Bridge, her specter still haunted the surface world.

"I have many names," answered the darkness.

Morgana's response snuffed out Angor Rot's torch and nearly brought him to his knees. Sensing the night sky brighten behind him, he turned and saw that the Black Sea had become purple. Judging by the waves' unnaturally slow movement, Angor Rot wondered if he had also stepped out of time when he stepped off his raft.

"I come to trade," he said, feeling dwarfed by the cave's looming mouth. "Gunmar's war for the surface lands has ravaged my village. I need the power to protect my people."

"You seek magic, but what do you bring in return?" asked Morgana.

What do I bring? What more could she possibly want? Angor Rot thought in disbelief.

Yet he could not turn away. Not now. Not after taking this painful journey. Not after sacrificing all he'd ever cherished, even his pet dove. Finding courage in his resolve, Angor Rot uncovered his dagger and dug it into his side. He winced as he cut out a piece of his stone flesh. With another spot of his soul now exposed, Angor Rot braved into the cavern.

"Here, my offering," Angor Rot said weakly. "Carved from my own living stone."

A long, slender arm sheathed in gold reached out of the shadows. Morgana's gilded fingernails clinked as they curled around the stone skin, claiming it. Her clutched fist shaped the flesh into something new. And when the hand opened, it revealed a ring.

Angor Rot's yellow eyes widened as incandescent orbs flew out of the ring and into his palm. They reminded him of the ones he'd once seen emerge from Deya the Deliverer's Amulet when the Trollhunter summoned her Daylight Sword.

"Yes!" cried Angor Rot in shock and gratitude. "I can . . . I can feel it! It is so . . . It is so . . ."

Flames the same color as his eyes spewed from Angor Rot's hands. In the resulting glow, he thought he actually glimpsed Morgana wearing a barbed headdress.

At last, thought Angor Rot, feeling a swell of renewed strength. *After all this loss, this hunting, I now have that which I need—POWER! The power to avenge my tribe against Gunmar. The power to ensure that no other village suffers as did mine!*

The yellow flames suddenly went out. Angor Rot gaped in surprise at his empty hands before doubling over in agony. Pain wracked his entire body, as if those orbs now burrowed deeper inside him. He vomited them out. When the orbs left his body, they took something else of Angor Rot's with them. He watched them return to Morgana's awaiting hand. The ring she had crafted now levitated, filled with whatever force the orbs had stolen from Angor Rot.

"My soul!" he screamed. "You lied to me!"

Morgana snickered and said, "You fool. Your flesh is worth nothing."

"What have you done to me?" demanded Angor Rot, his voice feeling as hollow as his chest. "Inside, I am so . . . so . . . empty!"

"I gave you what you wanted," said the sorceress. "Now your soul is mine!"

All Angor Rot had to show for this final offering, this ultimate theft, was Morgana's shrill laughter. That laughter followed him long after he floated away on his raft, regretting that he ever summoned Argante. Pale Lady. Baba Yaga. Eldritch Queen.

Morgana. Or as Angor Rot now felt compelled to call her . . . Master.

You will seek Merlin's champions and bring death to his Trollhunters, her voice echoed.

"No!" Angor Rot howled at the moon.

He cared not about Merlin or his champions. His quarrel had always been with Gunmar the Black. Yet, he could still sense his soul inside that ring—that Inferna Copula. Morgana's control over him was complete. He had no choice but to obey. But Angor Rot had also seen Deya the Deliverer in action. He knew that to defeat a Trollhunter, he would need an *edge*.

Once again the Black Sea turned purple. The raft stopped moving, as if anchored, and Morgana's golden arm reached out from the depths. The sight reminded Angor Rot of a legend he'd once heard about one of Merlin's allies. But unlike that Lady in the Lake, Morgana did not offer a sword. Instead, she gave Angor Rot a staff with an end as forked as her tongue.

Take the Skathe-Hrün, Angor Rot heard Morgana say in his mind.

The soulless Troll did as he was told, and the Shadow Staff became but the first of his many new possessions. At Izmir Trollmarket, Angor Rot swapped his raft for a Krubera-made digging vehicle known as a Borer. The two-headed Troll vendor didn't feel it was a fair trade—a battered dinghy for a diamond drill tank—but Angor Rot was long past fairness. Rather than beg or plea or quibble with lesser beings, he simply took what he wanted, just as his soul had been taken.

He traveled day and night to add to his growing arsenal, tunneling underground on the Borer to avoid deadly sunlight. He surfaced at Mecca and stole a batch of Creeper's Sun, to polish his dagger with the poison. Then, emerging again in Karachi, he took a hive of Pixies.

My *Pixies*, Angor Rot thought while strapping their hive to his back.

As the Borer took him to his next destination, it occurred to Angor Rot that he was no longer collecting animals, but weapons. The humble gamekeeper was gone. In his place now stood Angor Rot, the *assassin*.

Time lost all meaning as he navigated the globe, doing Morgana's bidding, seeking Merlin's champions. Angor Rot could only quiet the witch's voice in his head by hiding in the black portals cast by Skathe-Hrün. There, in the Shadow Realm, he was free to think, to plan.

Is this truly my fate? Angor Rot thought in darkness. *To endlessly hunt Morgana's prey one by one? Might my curse be lifted sooner if I instead hunt her* true *enemy—Merlin himself?*

And so Angor Rot arrived at the heart of a jungle in Ranthambore, India, and slipped into the Temple of the Pale One. The locals had named the structure after the solitary figure who lived within its walls. Sure enough, Angor Rot found the Pale One inside the temple, bearded and graying, wearing emerald armor similar in design to Morgana's.

"Hmm, I don't recall inviting you in here," said Merlin the Wizard.

"Then allow me to invite you into the shadows— for eternity," Angor Rot answered, opening a swirling black vortex with his staff.

Merlin sighed wearily and said, "You will suffer for what you've done, assassin."

"Ah, but to suffer, I would need a soul, wizard," sneered Angor Rot.

With Morgana's power coursing through his

body, he lunged at Merlin. The wizard dodged the attack and pointed to his left and right. With two pulling motions, Merlin wrenched heavy chains out of the walls. The iron manacles clamped around Angor Rot's wrists, knocking the Skathe-Hrün from his grasp. Merlin then brought his hands lower, and the chains dragged the assassin to the temple floor like a trapped animal.

"Release me, wizard!" Angor Rot shouted. "You cannot keep me captive. I am already indentured to another master!"

"Yes, I smell Morgana's horrendous handiwork in this," Merlin sneered. "Yet here you shall stay. Alone, with not even your miserable soul to keep you company in the meantime."

The wizard then reached upward and yanked at the air above him. Angor Rot heard a rumbling noise and looked up in time to see the temple ceiling cave in. Hundreds of tons of solid rock slabs rained down on Angor Rot, burying him under their crushing weight.

"For eternity," Merlin added after the last stone settled.

The exhausted wizard left the temple, never to

return. But Angor Rot did not hear Merlin's departing footsteps, just as he had not heard the avalanche hit him.

No, for the next several centuries, all Angor Rot heard was Morgana's bitter laugh and the innocent coo of his dear, departed dove. . . .

CHAPTER 1
BAPTISM BY LIAR

Jim Lake Jr. had the weirdest dream. In it, an old man trapped Jim in a little glass bottle. Jim pushed against the cork stopper with all his might, but his tiny arms and legs were useless, despite the Daylight Armor supporting them. The old man finally popped the cork, poured Jim into a giant Food Magic 3000, and pressed the frappé button. Jim thought he might have been screaming, but it was hard to tell over the whirring of the blender's oversized blades.

When the Trollhunter woke up from his dream, it wasn't a scream that escaped his lips—it was a flurry of bubbles. Jim's eyes snapped open, and he immediately felt cold pressure around his entire body. The good news was he wasn't trapped in a giant blender. But the bad news? Jim was trapped at the bottom of a giant body of water instead.

He yelped in alarm, releasing another shimmering wave of bubbles. The Trollhunter watched the last of his oxygen float to the surface, some fifty feet above. Feeling his emptied lungs burn, Jim tried to swim. But the Daylight Armor encasing his body only weighed him down. He disturbed the muck beneath his leaden boots, kicking up a cloud of silt.

Great, thought Jim. *Now I'm blind* and *drowning!*

Forcing himself not to panic, he reached for the Amulet on his chest and twisted it off. The metal breastplate to which it had been affixed vanished, as did the rest of the Daylight Armor. Now freed, and considerably lighter, Jim kicked his legs as hard as he could. He swam higher, even as his vision grew darker, and his head lighter. Jim felt the Amulet slip from his fingertips. He watched the device sink away, along with his hopes of survival.

The Trollhunter focused his last bit of willpower and reached out toward the Amulet. A bright blue glow appeared below and shot toward Jim like a rocket. He grabbed onto the Amulet as it passed, and the magic disc dragged him up and out of the water with a splash.

Now flying over the surface, Jim gasped for air. His daze lifted, and he thought he saw a pine forest backlit by the dusk—right before the Amulet reached the top of its arc. With another yelp, Jim started to fall. He crashed into the water again, only this part was much shallower. The Trollhunter trudged out of the lake and collapsed on its shore. Still catching his breath, he looked at the Amulet in his hand and said, "Would it have killed you to let me down gently?"

Ting! the Amulet chimed in response.

Jim shook the water from his ears. He looked at the canopy of silhouetted trees before recognizing the manmade dam at the opposite end of the lake.

I know this place! Jim thought. *Lake Arcadia Oaks. Tobes and I used to go camping here back when we were Junior Mole Scouts.*

A breeze blew through the pines, making Jim shiver. He wrapped his arms around his soaked body and lamented how this wasn't the first watery grave he'd avoided this week. But such narrow escapes were all too common for Jim lately. Ever since Merlin's Amulet transformed him into the first human Trollhunter, Jim's world had flipped from ordinary to extraordinary—not necessarily in a good way. Nothing but madness, misery, and mayhem followed. And that was just at high school. Jim didn't even want to think about all the near-beheadings, trials by combat, and exiles to infernal dimensions that came with his part-time job.

As he wrung out his sopping wet sweater, he tried to recall how he wound up at the bottom of a lake in the first place. The last thing the Trollhunter remembered was how Merlin prepared some potion in the Food Magic 3000 blender Jim's mom got him for his last birthday.

Well, hopefully not my last *birthday,* Jim mentally corrected himself. *Maybe I should just call it my most recent one. I'd like to live past my teens, if possible!*

But the thought did little to cheer Jim. Because it then made him think of the whole reason behind Merlin's elixir: the Eternal Night. Jim's Troll friends, Blinky and AAARRRGGHH!!!, had gone over the bullet points of this prophesied end of the world: If Gunmar used Merlin's Staff of Avalon to restore

Morgana to life, the crazy witch would bring about an everlasting eclipse. With no sunlight to turn them to stone, the evil Gumm-Gumms would dominate the entire planet, above and below. And the good Trolls and humans—humans like Jim's mom and best friends, Toby and Claire—well, they'd be hunted to extinction.

"If they're even alive now," Jim muttered, draining the water from his sneakers.

His memory gradually came back, and Jim felt a surge of worry for his loved ones. His mom, Barbara, had gone missing earlier that day, and Toby and Claire set out to search for her. But Jim still hadn't heard back from them, and that was hours ago—before the sun went down and Merlin cornered his latest Trollhunter with the strange brew he'd concocted.

Jim reached for his phone to check for any texts or voicemails. But his pockets were empty. He slapped his forehead in frustration, and the jolt jogged the missing bits of his recollection. Jim had left his cell by the bathroom sink, after he'd filled the tub with water and poured in the elixir. After he'd donned the Daylight Armor and submerged himself in the bath. After Merlin had told him that, to stop the Eternal Night, Jim would have to become both Troll *and* Hunter. . . .

"Whatever that means," Jim mumbled with another shiver.

He considered the darkening woods around him. Lake Arcadia Oaks was only a few miles outside town. Jim figured he could walk it. Especially since he couldn't use his ride-sharing app without a phone. But if Jim hustled, he might even make it back in time to whip up breakfast for his mom and friends—because they had to be okay, they just *had* to—and call out Merlin for the liar he was. After all, that elixir was supposed to transform Jim into something bigger and better, not teleport him way out to the boonies.

Jim soon heard a whining that was not his own. This one came from between a few of the tall, black pines. He walked over and peered into the woods. Jim heard another whine and spotted its source just a few feet ahead.

A small wolf pup with floppy ears and a gray-and-white coat lay between two fallen logs. Some old fishing line was tangled around his paws like a plastic net. And the more the puppy struggled, the more it constricted around him.

"Hang on, little guy," Jim said softly.

He knelt and gradually extricated the young wolf from the web of carelessly discarded garbage. As soon as he was free, the pup ran away.

"Uh, you're welcome?" said Jim in annoyance.

The pup stopped in his tracks and looked back. Jim stayed crouched and slowly offered out his hand. The wolf's big ears piqued in curiosity as he crept back and gave Jim a few tentative sniffs.

"There you go," said Jim in a sweet, singsong tone.

Feeling more at ease, the small wolf sat on his haunches and looked up at the Trollhunter. He started petting the pup, scratching behind his ear and saying, "I'd be worried that your mama is sizing me up for dinner right about now, but I'm guessing you're all alone out here. Me too."

The pup cocked his head at Jim and started barking, as if in answer.

"Geez, listen to Sir Barks-a-Lot over here," Jim joked.

Another gust blew through the woods, and

the trees creaked around them. Jim looked up at the sky, and saw moonlight filtering between the growing storm clouds. He stood up and said, "Well, later, Sir Barks."

Jim started heading to where he thought the main road was located. He'd only walked a few feet, when he heard another bark. Turning, Jim saw the pup behind him, tail wagging.

"Uh, you probably don't wanna go where I'm headed," Jim said. "I don't know what their feeling is about dogs, but Trolls sure think cats are delicious."

The Trollhunter resumed on his way, and Sir Barks followed. Jim tried to shoo him away, saying "Go on, skedaddle! Run free! Live *la vida lupa*!"

The wolf didn't budge an inch.

"Seriously, Sir Barks, you're better off keeping your distance," Jim pleaded, pulling the Amulet from his pocket. "Ever since this thing found me, my life's gotten pretty unpleasant—"

High above them, the thunderclouds parted, revealing a low, full moon—a Hunter's Moon. Jim's body suddenly seized with agony. It felt like his every nerve ending was on fire. He fell over, dropping the Amulet and startling Sir Barks. The wolf pup ran back to the trees. Jim was grateful, but not for the intense pain shooting through his muscles and bones that made his jaws clench, his eyes water.

Through his tears, Jim thought he saw something approach from the woods. It wasn't Sir Barks. It was a large, lumbering figure that soon became two. Jim couldn't tell if the double vision was due to his bleary eyes or if one body had been walking behind another. He fumbled for the Amulet, but his hands couldn't coordinate, wouldn't respond.

It was almost as if the Trollhunter's body wasn't his own anymore.

CHAPTER 2
A FISTFUL OF BEARD

"What—have—you—*done*?" asked Doctor Barbara Lake through gritted teeth. "I did *not* just escape that Dark Trollmarket only to be separated from my son all over again!"

"Well, technically, the boy did it to himself," Merlin began.

Barbara wasn't having any of it. She shoved the wizard against her bathroom wall with her forearm against his windpipe. He wheezed and said, "Perhaps I did play *some* small part. . . ."

She looked away from the bearded wizard in disgust and over to the tub. Inside, Barbara saw bathwater and the remnants of Merlin's elixir . . . but no Jim. Behind her, Toby Domzalski and Claire Nuñez stood by the bathroom's splintered doorjamb, trying to process what had happened to their best friend.

"I don't get it," said Toby. "One minute, we're out in the hallway, begging for Jim to let us into the bathroom. And not in a Taco Tuesday–related way!"

"We know he didn't use the door—we were too busy breaking it down," added Claire, her face almost as white as the streak in her hair. "And the window's locked from the inside. There's no other way Jim could've slipped past us."

"Not unless you count this fancy chamber pot," said Merlin, indicating the toilet.

Barbara pressed harder against the wizard and said, "Are you going to give us a straight answer? Or do I have to start breaking bones?"

"Trust me, Merlin, she knows how to do it," said Walter Strickler.

Jim's dapper former teacher had appeared behind Toby and Claire, consulting *The Book of Ga-Huel*. He flipped through the accursed pages and said, "Blast! This Gumm-Gumm tome is a record of the past, present, and future. Yet there's no mention in any of its chapters as to what might've happened to our young Atlas."

Barbara asked, "Claire, can't you use that shade stick to—?"

"It's called the Skathe-Hrün," Merlin corrected hoarsely, recognizing in Claire's hands the very same weapon Angor Rot once wielded against him.

Claire ignored the wizard and said, "Already on it, Dr. Lake."

She extended her Shadow Staff and concentrated on the space between its tines. A black hole opened, and Claire searched through it—not with her eyes, but with her heart. Toby and the others took a step back as the portal dilated, taking up half of the crowded bathroom. Claire's eyebrows knitted, but the vortex sputtered, then shrank into nothingness.

"I . . . I don't understand," said Claire. "Jim's always been my strongest emotional anchor. I know him so well, I could track him across the planet."

Barbara's eyes grew as she loosened her chokehold on Merlin. Strickler said, "Is it possible he ventured into the Darklands once more?"

"No way," Toby answered adamantly. "Jimbo promised he'd never go there again without us."

Merlin cleared his throat and said, "Rest assured, the Trollhunter remains on the surface world. Though his exact location escapes me, at the moment. . . ."

"But how could you be so reckless?" Strickler asked. "How could you expose him to something this unpredictable?"

"That's a bit like the cauldron calling the kettle black, isn't it, Changeling?" Merlin said.

Strickler's eyes flared yellow before the shape-shifter looked away in shame.

"Besides, unpredictability is the very essence of magic," the wizard continued while adjusting his emerald skullcap. "Worry not. He'll be fine."

Barbara laughed flatly and said, "Merlin, you may have had many champions, but you've clearly never been a parent. Worry comes with the job, especially when you have a kid as amazing I do. It's my responsibility to protect Jim. Not the other way around. But you've lost him, so now you're going to help *find* him."

Before Merlin could protest, Barbara grabbed a fistful of beard and dragged him out of the bathroom.

"OW!" was all the wizard could manage to say as they went downstairs.

Shrugging, Strickler turned to Claire and Toby and said, "Nomura has yet to report in. She may be under the misapprehension that Barbara and I are still Gunmar's prisoners. I'll make contact and have her search for Jim instead."

"While I spend some time in the Shadow Realm," said Claire, opening a new portal with her staff. "As much as that place makes my skin crawl, being cut off from outside distractions might 'signal boost' my connection to Jim—like a really freaky sensory deprivation tank."

Claire disappeared into the black hole, leaving Toby alone in the bathroom. He opened the window and said, "I guess that makes me in charge of aerial surveillance!"

Toby got a running start and jumped out the window. Normally, this would be a problem for anyone escaping a second-story bathroom. But Toby's Warhammer activated at once, halting him in midair. He floated higher and higher above Jim's house, scanning their neighborhood like a human drone. Toby saw his own home across the cul-de-sac, Claire's place two blocks away, and Main Street just beyond that. Thunder rumbled overhead, and

Toby became aware of the storm gathering on the horizon. He gulped nervously and said, "Aw, Jimbo. I sure wish Blinky and AAARRRGGHH!!! were here. They'd know what to do."

"I have absolutely no idea what to do!" shouted Blinky. "Other than—RUN!"

The six-eyed Troll ducked the Parlok Spear that was aimed for his head and broke into a sprint across the Quagawump Swamps. AAARRRGGHH!!! galloped on all fours after him, swatting away another incoming volley of spears and grumbling, "Good plan."

"After them!" commanded Queen Usurna, her feathered crown trembling. "The Eternal Night must proceed quickly, or Gunmar will add all our skulls to his throne!"

Krubera soldiers chased after the fleeing Trolls. Blinky looked back at them and said, "And here I thought the worst thing about this place was its music!"

"Boom, boom, shake the room, say whaaaaa?" sang AAARRRGGHH!!!

The tune made Blinky think of happier times

and he smiled, despite the spears whizzing past him and AAARRRGGHH!!! Had it only been a few months ago when they first escorted Claire, Tobias, and Master Jim to the Quagawump Swamps? Their team had been in search of the second Triumbric Stone needed to defeat Gunmar, and the Wumpas were initially hostile to all foreigners. But in deposing their false king and restoring order, Team Trollhunters had believed they'd made friends for life with the grateful Wumpas. It was the very reason for Blinky and AAARRRGGHH!!!'s latest visit here. They believed the Wumpa Queen would be more than willing to pledge her forces to the Trollhunters' cause—to band together to join an army large enough to thwart the Eternal Night.

"Heads up," warned AAARRRGGHH!!!

He snatched another spear out of the air before it harpooned Blinky, and hurled it back to its sender. The weapon skewered the Gumm-Gumm who had first thrown it, turning him into a lifeless stone statue.

"You have my thanks, as ever, Aarghaumont," Blinky said in gratitude. "Just as I would have thanked the Wumpas not to ambush us!"

For no sooner had Blinky and AAARRRGGHH!!! returned with their plea for aid, than the Wumpa Queen revealed they'd been beaten to the punch— by Usurna and her dedicated squad of murderous Kruberas. The betrayal irked Blinky to no end, but he realized there were more pressing concerns at the moment.

"Look, old friend!" said Blinky, pointing his four arms straight ahead. "A fire bog!"

AAARRRGGHH!!! nodded and hefted Blinky onto his mossy back. The musclebound Troll bent his legs and jumped with all his might, carrying both of them over a field of smoking peat. They landed clear on the other side, and the pursuing Kruberas had no choice but to race after them.

As soon as they set foot on the bog, jets of flame shot out from the ground. The intense heat burned the Kruberas, keeping them at bay . . . for now. Blinky and AAARRRGGHH!!! took off again. After putting some distance between themselves and Usurna's scorched soldiers, they rested in a cave far off the beaten path.

"Great Gizmodius, what a week!" Blinky exclaimed, catching his breath. "As our human friends might say, I am royally cheesed off!"

"Royal cheese sauce?" asked AAARRRGGHH!!! uncertainly.

"No, no, 'royally cheesed off,'" Blinky corrected. "It's a surface world expression that means . . . oh, it doesn't matter what it means! We've landed in a most hopeless predicament this time—and in our line of work, that's really saying something!"

"Not all bad," said AAARRRGGHH!!!

Blinky followed his teammate's gaze and saw a series of deep pools glowing within their shelter. Together, they peered into one of the pools and saw their own burdened reflections on the surface . . . until its waters rippled, seemingly disturbed from within.

"How odd," Blinky said. "It's almost as if the pool responded to our emotions."

"Troubled waters," AAARRRGGHH!!! grunted in understanding.

"Just so, old friend," Blinky agreed with mounting worry. "Though our fate appears most dire at present, I somehow feel an even *greater* concern for our allies. Especially Master Jim . . ."

CHAPTER 3
STAR-CROSSED SHOVERS

Before he opened his eyes, Jim heard the crackle of flames. He smelled at least two different kinds of wood burning—oak and some kind of pine. Jim didn't know how his nose could distinguish such subtle scents in the smoke. It never could before.

He sat up and looked around the lakeshore. A bonfire flickered in front of him. It warmed Jim's body, which no longer throbbed with pain. All he felt now was soreness in his muscles . . . and tightness in his clothes. Jim figured the combination of the lake water and heat must've shrunk his sweater and jeans.

Sir Barks-a-Lot sprang from the nearby woods, followed by two Trolls. The wolf pup jumped on Jim, who recognized the Trolls' silhouettes as the ones he saw before passing out cold. They dumped the logs in their arms onto the bonfire. In the rising glow, Jim saw that one of them was a Garden Troll, flowers blooming in a delicate crown from her head branches. The other clearly hailed from the River Tribe, given the large, squat boulder atop his skull. Once they noticed Jim was awake, the Garden Troll clapped her hands together excitedly and said, "Look, Ronagog! The human isn't dead after all! Can we keep him? Can we?"

"I dunno, Junipra," answered Ronagog the River Troll. "You think he's cave-broken? 'Cause I'm not cleaning up any of his 'accidents'!"

"Excuse me," said Jim as he stood on unsteady legs. "I'm not going to be your pet."

"Oh. So, you're not cave-broken," said Junipra, looking crestfallen. "I guess *that's* why his clothes were drenched when we found him."

"No!" yelled Jim. "I mean, yes, I'm 'cave-broken'! I haven't wet myself since I was in preschool. Well, maybe a *little* the first time I laid eyes on Bular. . . ."

Ronagog gasped and said, "You've seen the son of Gunmar? And lived to tell of it?"

"Well, yeah, but—" Jim began before Junipra shoved Ronagog.

"Aw, are you scared?" teased the Garden Troll.

"So what if I am?" asked Ronagog, pushing back.

"Stop!" yelled the Trollhunter. "There's no need to fight like this!"

Junipra and Ronagog stopped tussling and gave Jim a confused look.

"'Fight'?" Ronagog repeated. "This isn't a fight, fleshling. It's our courtship dance!"

"Look how cute the incontinent human is when he's confused!" said Junipra. "This is how we show affection in Troll culture. We're in love!"

"Oh, I know what you're thinking," Ronagog said to Jim.

"I seriously doubt that," Jim muttered with a shake of his head.

"She's a 'grubby Garden Troll,' and I'm a 'rotten River Troll'!" Ronagog went on, winking at Junipra in some a private joke. "We've heard it all before. How we're crazy. How us being together is forbidden by our feuding tribes."

"Yeah, about that feud," said Jim. "It's ancient history. My friends and I just—"

"Exactly—ancient history!" Junipra cut in. "That's what *we've* been saying! But our elders are sooooo old-fashioned. And Ronagog and I . . . we can't fight what's in our hearts. Do you have any idea what that feels like?"

"I . . . I think I do," Jim said softly.

The Trollhunter looked up at the stars glittering between the clouds and wondered if Claire was doing the same. The brightest points in the constellations reminded Jim of her eyes, of the streak in her hair, of her perfect white teeth whenever she smiled at him. He flashed back to the first time he saw Claire, when their moms chatted at some city fundraiser in Barbara's hospital. Jim then winced, recalling his pathetic attempts months later to "unleash his Español" and talk to her. But then he allowed himself to smile, remembering the first time she made him guacamole, the first time they slow-danced at the lookout point, the first time Claire called Jim her "boyfriend."

"'O, swear not by the moon, th' inconstant moon,'" Jim whispered to himself. "'That monthly changes in her circle orb, lest that thy love prove likewise variable.'"

"That's beautiful," said Junipra, overhearing. "Is it from the Venerable Bedehilde?"

"No, the venerable Shakespeare," said Jim.

The line came back to him, one of many Jim and Claire had rehearsed for Ms. Janeth's high school production of *Romeo and Juliet*. At the time, he'd worried he'd never be able to remember all that dialogue, but Claire always found a way to make Jim believe in himself. Jim sighed and wished he could hold Claire's hand in his . . . his surprisingly hairy hand.

"Whoa! Where'd *that* come from?!" Jim blurted out.

Sir Barks and the two shoving Trolls looked at him. He inspected the wiry hairs sprouting from his knuckles, so black they were almost blue. Those weren't there yesterday. Neither were Jim's long fingernails, which looked as though they hadn't been clipped in months.

Have I been so busy Trollhunting, I forgot about basic grooming? Jim thought. *Maybe my dad was a hairy guy too. I barely remember him, but I'm pretty sure he wasn't a yeti!*

Sir Barks started growling, and Jim saw the hackles on the puppy's back rise. Ronagog and Junipra stopped wrestling and turned to the woods, where several Garden Trolls emerged.

"Mother! Father!" Junipra said to her tribe's oldest members. "What brings you here?"

"Preventing you from making a terrible mistake!" answered Junipra's father. "Remove your hands from my daughter, river riffraff—lest I remove them from your wrists!"

"How dare you speak to our son that way, garden garbage!" shouted someone from behind.

Jim saw a handful of River Trolls wade out of the lake. Ronagog let go of Junipra and said to them, "Please, parents, stay out of this! I'm old enough to make my own decisions!"

"Decisions that bring shame to our entire tribe!" declared Ronagog's mother. "Or have you forgotten our blood feud with Garden Trolls since time immemorial?"

Jim jumped between both camps and yelled, "WAIT! Everyone relax for a second. My friends and I ended that feud a few days ago. But I'm guessing you guys didn't get the memo. . . ."

"I got your memo right here!" hollered a River Troll before he punched a Garden Troll.

And just like that, a new minifeud erupted between them on the banks of Lake Arcadia Oaks.

Sir Barks-a-Lot ducked behind Jim's legs, poking between them every so often to yap at the fighting Trolls. Hanging his head in disappointment, Jim pulled the Amulet from his shrunken pocket and read the incantation engraved on its back.

"'For the glory of Merlin, Daylight is mine to command!'"

In a swirl of mist and magic, the pieces of the Daylight Armor materialized around Jim. Sir Barks whimpered as the silver plates snapped together and electric blue energy blazed along their etched patterns. Phosphorescent orbs shot like emergency flares from the Amulet now on Jim's breastplate, forming the Daylight Sword in his hand.

Suited for battle, the Trollhunter took one step toward the tribes—and promptly collapsed. His body lurched with another round of muscle-knotting spasms. Jim cried out. Sir Barks circled him protectively, alternately whining in sympathy and barking to scare away whatever afflicted his human friend. Hearing the commotion, some of the Garden and River Trolls broke away from the fight and considered the bizarre, trembling human going into shock at their feet.

"My pet!" exclaimed Junipra, pulling away from her parents. "I think he's sick!"

"He alone understands the love Junipra and I feel for each other!" Ronagog hollered from the lake, where his family had dragged him.

"Then he's every bit as abominable as your unspeakable union!" hissed Junipra's father.

The cluster of Garden and River Trolls started stomping on Jim's armored form. Sir Barks bit at their heels, trying to drag them away, until a much louder growl drowned out his own. The Trolls looked down right before their bodies were sent flying with a furious roar. The echo carried across the lake and made Sir Barks hide his head under his paws. Every Garden and River Troll gasped as the Trollhunter snarled back at them, Jim's teeth sharpened into fangs, his eyes redder than blood.

CHAPTER 4
THE WEAPON WHO WALKS

In all his lifetimes, Angor Rot had never witnessed anything that filled him with as much wonder and dread as he now felt. Not when Merlin buried him in an avalanche at the Temple of the Pale One. Not when that fool Strickler freed him centuries later, only to switch sides, as all Changelings did. Not when that human girl stole his Skathe-Hrün and the Trollhunter finally put Angor Rot out of his misery. Not even when Morgana's spirit recently resurrected her assassin, only to condemn him to another existence of supernatural servitude.

For Angor Rot's yellow eye now looked upon the one, true Morgana. Her gaunt, golden form hovered over the remains of her prison for the past millennia: Dark Trollmarket's corrupted Heartstone.

Angor Rot felt the irresistible urge to kneel before the sorceress in spite of his conflicted emotions. Doing so, he looked to the side and saw Gunmar— the Gumm-Gumm Angor Rot despised above all others, the merciless monster with whom Angor Rot was now forced to conspire—also bowing his horned head.

"The Eternal Night is here," announced Morgana.

The sorceress's heels clicked on the Heartstone's shards as she lowered herself. Gunmar stood with haste, clearly uncomfortable bending to any master. He said, "You speak the words my black heart has longed to hear for so very long, Pale Lady. Every war I've won, every life I've ended, has led to this, the surface world's last rites. I, Gunmar the Vicious, the Skullcrusher, the Warbringer will ready my armies at once to—"

"No," Morgana interrupted, her voice like an icicle.

Angor Rot now felt another urge—the urge to laugh—as Gunmar's single eye flared in insult. The gilded witch floated, surveying all of Dark Trollmarket. Thousands upon thousands of Gumm-Gumm soldiers stood at the ready with their barbaric armor and weapons.

"Before I extinguish the sun, you must first tie up all loose ends," Morgana said while eying the countless Trolls at her disposal.

"I do not permit 'loose ends,'" Gunmar replied in defiance.

"Don't you?" she asked. "Then what shall we call the Changeling and the human woman who escaped after you bade them release me?"

"The *Impure* and the Trollhunter's mother are of no consequence," Gunmar said dismissively.

"But their knowledge *is*," said Angor Rot, relishing the Gumm-Gumm's outrage. "Who knows the amount of sensitive information to which they might have been exposed? Before you let them *escape*, that is. . . ."

He felt Gunmar's furious eye boring into the back of his neck, while Morgana said, "Ah, Angor Rot, as observant as he is relentless. It would seem I chose wisely when remaking you into my champion, my weapon who walks."

"A weapon that's dulled with age," sneered Gunmar. "Angor Rot was unable to slay those you consider 'loose ends' when he had the chance months ago."

The Gumm-Gumm flexed his right claw, and faint wisps rose from his veins—veins that glowed gold with the life force leeched from the dying Heartstone. The gossamer strands gathered and coalesced into the Decimaar Blade. But rather than turn the smoldering weapon upon Angor Rot, Gunmar crossed to the other side of the cavern, where a trio of Stalklings awaited him. He dragged the searing tip against all three Vulture Trolls' necks, and their eyes instantly glazed over like mirrored chrome.

"The Stalklings' sight is now my own, as are their minds," said Gunmar. "They shall soar over Arcadia and eliminate the Trollhunter and his ilk—"

He hesitated under Morgana's withering glare before adding, "—*if* it pleases my Eldritch Queen."

The sorceress nodded her spiked head in approval. The Gumm-Gumm king shoved his Stalklings' reins into Angor Rot's hands. Leaning close so Morgana wouldn't hear, Gunmar said, "Lead them up the crystal stairs, then out via the Horngazel tunnel. I suspect even a lapdog like you could handle so simple a task. After all, didn't you once have animals of your own?"

Angor Rot still seethed after he'd unleashed the Stalklings at the Arcadia Oaks dry canal. Perhaps Morgana would not punish her weapon if he walked into Dark Trollmarket and drove his poison dagger into Gunmar's back. She might even reward Angor Rot with his long-lost freedom for ridding the world of the arrogant Gumm-Gumm.

But deep down, Angor Rot knew Morgana would never free his soul. He was about to trudge back down the Horngazel's swirling tunnel of rock and light when the wind shifted. Angor Rot's sharpened senses detected a scent on the night air, one that seemed at once familiar and *unfamiliar*. It belonged to the only other being he despised as much as Gunmar.

"Trollhunter . . . ," said Angor Rot as he let the Horngazel close behind him and walked toward the coming storm.

CHAPTER 5
GROWING PAINS

Despite the many differences between them, every Garden and River Troll around Lake Arcadia Oaks stared with the same amazed expression at the feral Trollhunter. Seeing the surprise on the faces of those who had just ganged up on him, Jim regained his senses. His irises faded to their normal blue. He took a breath and said, "Com dwhon, evweywon."

Jim appeared as bewildered by what he just said as everyone else. Even Sir Barks cocked an ear in confusion. He meant to say *Calm down, everyone*, but the words came out garbled. Jim ran his tongue over his teeth, feeling sharp fangs sprouting from his gums, and understood why.

"Why do you all stand there?" Ronagog's father said. "He's still a fleshbag!"

"On this—and only this—do we agree, River Troll!" added Junipra's mother. "This is a personal matter involving our children. Now the human must pay a price for his interference!"

Spurred by their elders, the Garden and River Trolls resumed their attack on Jim. But this time he was ready. The hairs on the back of his neck stood on end, sensing movement in the background. Jim could tell a River Troll was charging behind him, as he saw another do the same in front of him.

Bending at the knees, the Trollhunter waited until the last possible second, and then sprang into the air. His armored body jumped higher than it ever had, easily avoiding the two River Trolls. Unable to stop in time, they collided headfirst, cracking each other's boulders.

Jim landed gracefully on his feet, just like one of Nana Domzalski's many cats. A handful of Garden Trolls now encircled him, prodding their branch-horns at the Trollhunter. Thinking fast, he stuck the end of his Daylight Sword into the shore and then kicked it forward, spraying sand into the Garden Trolls' eyes, briefly blinding them.

Jim put his sword onto his back, then summoned

the Glaives from his thigh-plates. With one fluid motion he connected the interlocking blades and flung them. They spun in a wide arc, trimming off the tips of the Garden Trolls' branches before returning to Jim. He caught the Glaives and said, "Back off. Or you'll get another pwuning."

Pruning, Jim thought. *That would've sounded way cooler if I could actually say "pruning"!*

Either way, it worked. The snipped Garden Trolls returned to their elders, just as the recovering River Trolls rejoined theirs in the lake's shallows. Jim saw Junipra and Ronagog look longingly at each other from their parents' clutches and said, "Let 'em go. Please."

Hey, I can say my Ls again, thought Jim. *So there's some good news!*

Awed by the Trollhunter's victory over their tribes, the Garden and River elders released their children. Ronagog and Junipra embraced in the middle of the beach, their bodies lit by the wavering bonfire.

"Follow your foolish heart if you must, my child," said Junipra's father as the Garden Trolls retreated into the woods.

"But know that, from this moment forward, you

belong to neither of our tribes," added Ronagog's mother before the River Trolls sank back under the lake.

Junipra and Ronagog pulled apart, saddened by the finality of their parents' words. Jim felt bad for the two Trolls, only to be stricken by the onset of a throbbing headache. He staggered to the lake and studied his reflection on its rippling surface. The Trollhunter barely recognized the face that stared back at him. The tips of Jim's new fangs jutted past his lips. Dark hair hung over his eyes, looking far longer and shaggier than it did when he woke up that morning. And Jim couldn't tell if it was due to the pale moonlight or if he was still in shock, but his mottled skin now bore a faint, blueish tint.

What have I done? Jim wondered of his own distorted reflection. *Why did I let Merlin turn me into some . . . some weirdo human-Troll hybrid?*

Jim examined his new features in the lake, wondering how his mom and friends would react to his new face. Would they gasp, as the Garden and River Trolls did? Would they hide their eyes, unable to look at him? Or would they try real hard—too hard, even—to pretend that nothing was different at all?

Why, Toby would probably try to lighten the mood with a joke about "Jimbo 2.0" or something. Jim suddenly felt like he couldn't breathe. He stumbled away from the lake, and Sir Barks, Ronagog, and Junipra ran to his aid.

"Oh, my poor pet! Were you injured in battle?" asked Junipra.

"No," Jim choked, tugging at his collar. "Can't—get—air!"

The Trollhunter felt like he was trapped in a tin can, like the ones full of anchovies he used when cooking pasta putanesca. The Daylight Armor clamped so tightly around his body—even tighter than his clothes had minutes ago—that Jim's lungs couldn't even fill with oxygen. He wished he could trade in his suit for one that was at least two sizes bigger.

And just like that, the Daylight Armor restructured itself. Waves of energy radiated out of the Amulet and down the silver plates, causing them to expand and glide into new configurations. Jim watched his armor adjust, as it had done when he first wore it in his backyard those many months ago. Only then the suit shrank from Kanjigar the

Courageous's dimensions down to Jim's slender size. Now, though, the Daylight Armor grew again to accommodate Jim's increased height and muscle mass. The last metallic panel fastened into place, and the Trollhunter drew breath once more. He felt the fitted armor rise and fall with his own chest, perfectly tailored to Jim's new body.

"We can never thank you enough," Ronagog said. "Fighting for our love like that."

Junipra held Ronagog's hand and said, "Yet I suspect the *real* fight has only begun, now that our families have disowned us. If you have any inkling as to where we should go, Trollhunter, we'd greatly welcome it."

Jim stared at the smitten Trolls. Despite their large size, they seemed so vulnerable, so lost, even though they were together. He looked away from Ronagog and Junipra and to the shroud of storm clouds above them. His enhanced eyes focused on the moon, and Jim became aware that it wasn't the only "inconstant" thing in his life. Ever since he'd inherited the Amulet, Jim experienced one drastic change after another, going from student to Merlin's champion to . . . to the abominable Were-Troll he was now becoming. Could Jim and Claire ever hope to truly be together like Ronagog and Junipra? How would their relationship survive beyond high school, let alone the Eternal Night?

"I . . . I don't know what to tell you," he finally said. "It's like you made this choice without fully considering the consequences. And now you don't fit in at your old home anymore. So, it's hard to imagine where you're supposed to go next, when you don't even know where you belong in the first place."

Jim finished, unsure if those words were meant for the pair of Trolls . . . or for himself. Junipra's and Ronagog's eyes rounded with sorrow, and she asked, "Are . . . are you saying we'd be better off *alone*?"

"Maybe," said Jim. "Maybe that's the right thing to do when we really care about someone—cut them loose before our decisions come back to hurt the ones we love."

Ronagog and Junipra nodded solemnly and unlaced their fingers. The Garden Troll shook her flower-crowned head and said, "All I ever want is for you to be happy, dear Ronagog. . . ."

"And I you, my beloved Junipra," said Ronagog,

his eyes misting with tears. "But given the bitter history between our tribes, perhaps that happiness will only be found a . . . a . . ."

"Apart," sobbed Junipra, finishing the sentence that Ronagog could not.

The forlorn Garden and River Trolls shared one final, weak smile before turning their backs on each other and heading off in separate directions. Jim watched them go, until he was left with his own sorrow—and Sir Barks-a-Lot.

"You better take off too, little guy," Jim said, pushing the wolf pup away with the toe of his boot.

But Sir Barks remained in place, even when thunder clashed over their heads. Jim shut his eyes and grimaced, the rumbling only adding to the headache pounding at his temples. A light rain fell on the Trollhunter. Lightning raked across the sky.

And in that brief, strobing flash, Angor Rot stood illuminated at the edge of the woods, his weapons drawn, his yellow eye burning like a predator's.

CHAPTER 6
N IS FOR NO, M IS FOR MERCY

More ill winds swept across Arcadia, signaling the storm to come. Behind Stuart Electronics, newspapers blew like tumbleweeds past two tiny figures. Gnome Chompsky held on to his hat so the wind wouldn't take it. Beside him, NotEnrique balled his little Changeling fists and said, "Whattaya know about the missin' Trollhunter?"

Fragwa, the Goblin leader they'd cornered in the narrow alley, stroked his magic marker mustache and yelled, "Shik shaka!"

"Neep neep, neep neep neep," Chompsky responded impatiently.

"I agree," said NotEnrique. "I think the little scamp's holdin' out too."

"Shik shaka!" Fragwa yelled again, making rude

gestures with his fingers and toes.

"Oh, ya wanna do it the hard way, do ya?" NotEnrique threatened. "Fine. I'll play 'good cop,' while me Gnome pal here plays 'bad cop.'"

Chompsky hissed at the Goblin, revealing his miniature mouthful of serrated teeth. The Goblin stopped laughing and backed away, but the alley's brick wall blocked him. NotEnrique crossed his arms and smiled as the Gnome started throttling Fragwa. Desperate to end the interrogation, the Goblin grabbed the Talk 'n' Type toy at his side and started pressing its keys.

"N is for no. P is for please," said the toy's electronic voice. "M is for mercy."

"Now we're gettin' somewhere," NotEnrique said. "All right, spill yer guts!"

Fragwa opened his mouth to speak, but instead of words coming out, a glowing green rock flew in. The Goblin swallowed the foreign object in surprise, only for his body to spontaneously combust a second later. Stunned and splashed in green goo, Chompsky and NotEnrique turned around. At the other end of the alley, Steve Palchuk and Eli Pepperjack struck an over-the-top pose with their slingshots and more glowing Dwärkstone grenades.

"C is for Creepslayer," said Eli in his deepest, most dramatic voice.

"And that was for pepper-spraying me and Pepperjack, snot stain!" Steve hollered at the puddle that used to be Fragwa.

NotEnrique wiped the Goblin slime off his diaper and said, "That 'snot stain' was just about ta say somethin' that coulda helped us find the Trollhunter, ya glorks!"

"NEEP!" Chompsky shouted in rage at the Creepslayerz.

NotEnrique took a step away from his Gnome companion, saying, "Okay, easy there, fella. No need for *that* kinda language!"

"We were just trying to help!" Eli said. "And it's not like you can trust Goblins. My allowance is *still* paying for the damage they did to my mom's car!"

"Ah, who asked for yer help anyway?" NotEnrique groused.

"We did," said a female voice behind them.

NotEnrique, Chompsky, and the Creepslayerz watched Claire, Toby, and Strickler step out of another black hole and into the alley. Toby and

Claire each wore sleek new suits of Merlin-made armor—his reddish-brown, hers purple—and held their Warhammer and Shadow Staff at the ready. Claire closed her portal and added, "With Jim missing and Morgana finally freed, we're calling in every favor we can to keep Arcadia from going crazy-town banana-pants."

"Though Nomura still hasn't responded to my alerts," Strickler said. "I fear we may be down another member."

"Then we better not lose any more," Toby said— right before two pairs of claws snatched him and Claire high into the sky.

The abruptness of the abduction knocked the weapons from their hands. Strickler looked up from the Warhammer and Shadow Staff at his feet and saw two Vulture Trolls speeding away with Toby and Claire, followed by a third.

"I am getting so *sick* of Stalklings," said Strickler, reverting to his green, scaly Changeling form.

The Creepslayerz' eyes bugged as their one-time teacher threw back his cloak. He proceeded to unfurl his *own* set of wings. As he launched after Toby and Claire, one of Strickler's wings accidentally slapped Steve in the face during takeoff.

"Ew! Ew! Ew! Some of old man Strickler's wing skin got into my mouth!" Steve gagged, while Eli fainted beside him.

CHAPTER 7
THE ULTIMATE GAME

Sir Barks-a-Lot's barking did not help Jim's migraine. But at least it kept him alive. Like some canine alarm system, the pup spotted Angor Rot a second before he burst from the darkness. And that second was all the Trollhunter needed to instinctively tuck and roll into a defensive crouch. Jim pulled the Daylight Sword from his back, and another flicker of lightning revealed the assassin's leering face.

"Ah, but you *have* changed," Angor Rot taunted. "The Trollhunter I faced in Merlin's Tomb never moved so swiftly. Nor did your ally. What was his name again? Oh yes. *Draal.*"

Jim clumsily stood to his full height, inches taller than he was mere minutes ago. He did not take his eyes from the Troll circling around him.

Rain poured in sheets on them, matting Jim's wild mane and Sir Barks's fur.

"If you're trying to get a rise out of me, it won't work," Jim said. "I've already made my peace with Draal's death. Merlin saw to that."

"Yes, I can tell the geriatric wizard's been busy," Angor Rot replied. "Molding you. Shaping you. *Altering* you. This is what masters do to their champions, you see. They break us down, only to rebuild us according to their terrible design!"

"I'm nothing like you!" Jim shouted as he charged at Angor Rot.

The mercenary Troll anticipated the strike. He sidestepped Jim's sword and kicked his armored back, sending Jim face-first into a tree. Feeling like his skull had split open from the impact, he touched his forehead. Jim was certain he'd find blood mixed with the rain on his gauntlets. Instead, the Trollhunter felt two bony lumps protruding from his temples. And his headache finally disappeared.

"Are you quite certain?" Angor Rot asked from behind him. "For are we not both empowered by magical beings? Dispatched to do their bidding? Giving up pieces of ourselves along the way until there's nothing left but a shell of our former selves?"

Jim used the tree's trunk to pull himself up, and Sir Barks sprinted over to lick his wounds. He gave the wolf pup a stern look, and the meaning was clear: *Stay*.

"Hmm, perhaps we are different," Angor Rot said. "Even now, you betray your own weakness, putting the needs of lesser beings before your own. I long ago learned to rid myself of such pointless compassions. They are but burdens that slow our killing strokes."

"I'd take those 'burdens' over killing any day," said Jim, his voice stronger now. "That's your problem, Angor Rot. You've been dealing in death for so long, you've forgotten what it's like to live."

Angor Rot switched his dagger to his other hand and said, "Welcome to the ultimate game, boy—where hunter *hunts* hunter!"

He slashed at Jim. Only this time, it was the Trollhunter who anticipated the attack. With his head now clear, Jim found his senses heightened. Time seemed to slow as Angor Rot's blade sliced toward him. All at once, Jim could hear its razor-sharp edge sing through the air, smell the Creeper's

Sun poison coating its metal, and count the raindrops between them one by one.

Jim moved so quickly, he looked like a blur. He twirled his Daylight Sword in one hand, knocking aside the dagger, while delivering a punishing uppercut to Angor Rot's jaw with the other. The Troll reeled from the blow. He rubbed his chin, and a chunk of rotten stone—knocked loose by Jim's punch—broke off.

"Yes, earn your horns!" said Angor Rot. "Fight like a Troll before you die like one!"

He pulled a pouch from the leather strap across his chest and breathed in its contents. Plumes of black dust swirled up both nostrils, and his yellow eyes widened.

Grave Sand, thought Jim, recognizing the crushed Gumm-Gumm bones used to exaggerate a Troll's aggression.

With renewed vigor, Angor Rot ran shrieking toward the Trollhunter. The dagger and Daylight Sword clanged together, giving off sparks that sizzled in the rain. Sir Barks yipped in warning as Jim and Angor Rot faced off, their weapons locked in a fierce metal X between them.

"Tough talk from a two-time loser, Rot," said Jim through his gnashed fangs. "You got your soulless butt handed to you by Merlin in ye olden times— before my friends and I did the exact same thing!"

Angor Rot head-butted the Trollhunter between their blades. Jim expected the blow to hurt a lot more than it did. But Angor Rot's skull must've glanced off his growing horns.

"Alas, I came back, and that is where our similarities end, Trollhunter!" said Angor Rot. "When I kill you, it shall be permanent! You'll experience no rebirth at Merlin's hand or any other. And once I wipe my blade clean of your blood, I'll hunt down those you love! Tell me, does your dear, sweet mother still live in the same home?"

The threat exposed a new feeling within Jim. It went far beyond human concepts of rage. For most of his life, Jim Lake Jr. tried to behave, to mind his manners and be polite. But whatever emotional filters he'd built over time finally broke, just as the two horns broke the flesh on his scalp. The Trollhunter unleashed a primal cry. The howl echoed across Lake Arcadia Oaks, startling Sir Barks—and Angor Rot.

Jim fanned his shield and banged it into his ene-my's exposed side, knocking the wind out of him. Jim sent him upright again with an armored knee to the face. He followed with a flurry of jabs and kicks, not so much softening up his Troll punching bag as toying with him. Jim discovered a newfound, feral glee even in the middle of this life-or-death fight. He then gripped the handle of his Daylight Sword with both hands and swung with all his might.

Angor Rot managed to step back just in time as the sword cut through his chest strap. With the leather strap severed, the Pixie hive fell and landed in the mud behind him. Jim swept the off-balance Troll's feet out from under him with a final kick. Angor Rot fell backward, his spine smashing open the hive, his Grave Sand spilling out in a black cloud.

The Pixies escaped their shattered prison in luminous zig-zag patterns and flew through the powdered Gumm-Gumm bones. It made them buzz faster and brighter. Having encountered Pixies before, Jim commanded the helmet to appear over his head while cupping his hands over Sir Barks's nose, mouth, and ears. The Pixies pelted against

Jim's armored helmet and hands, but could not worm into any exposed orifices. Riled by the impenetrable armor, the insane insects spiraled off in the other direction. As they went, the Pixies whisked up the sack of Grave Sand, ferrying it away on their collective backs.

Jim watched them disappear into the thunderheads—only to realize that Angor Rot had disappeared too. Safe now, he released the grateful Sir Barks and vanished his helmet.

"That's right, Angor Rot! RUN!" shouted the Trollhunter before he gave another savage roar and chased after his prey.

CHAPTER 8
LOCAL LUNATICS

"That's the problem with a full moon—brings out all the crazies," said Detective Scott.

He hunted and pecked on his computer keyboard, while Barbara craned her neck to look out his office window. It offered a clear view of the Arcadia Oaks Police Department, which appeared alarmingly busy for seven p.m. on a Thursday night.

"I've seen them!" ranted a deranged man at the booking desk. "They fell from the sky! With their glowing skin! And arms! Lots of arms! But now they could be any of us!"

Two uniformed officers dragged the raving madman toward the holding cells. Along the way, they passed the precinct's waiting area, where an incredibly bored Merlin sat. Instead of his usual emerald armor, he now wore high-top sneakers, baggy para-chute pants, a PAPA SKULL LIVE IN CONCERT '92 T-shirt, sunglasses, and a porkpie hat. The wizard looked nuts, but those clothes were the only ones in Barbara's house that fit him.

"Yeah, I see what you mean, Detective Scott," Barbara said.

"Oh please, call me Louis," he said. "I mean, we should be on a first-name basis if we're in the same theater company, right?"

"Right," sighed Barbara, still regretting the exten-sive lie she told him to protect Jim's Trollhunting secret. "Look, Louis, I know someone needs to be gone for at least forty-eight hours before the police can file a missing person's report, but—"

"Hey, as a fellow parent, I get it," Detective Scott said. "If my Darci went somewhere without telling me where she was going—*and* left her cell phone behind—I'd be worried too. Then again, some of the things Darci's told me about Jim's behavior at school are also worrying. Failing grades, poor attendance, mood swings where he's incredibly cocky one day, fast asleep in Señor Uhl's Spanish class the next . . . and then there's *this*."

Detective Scott swiveled his monitor so that Barbara could see it. The screen showed Jim and Toby's mugshots from the time they were booked for breaking into the Museum of Arcadia. Barbara's heart sank.

"I'm sorry, but all this paints a picture of a very irresponsible young man," Detective Scott said in sympathy. "And don't get me started on Domzalski."

"Louis, I realize there's no way you could possibly understand this, but my son is the most responsible human being I know," said Barbara.

"Okay," Detective Scott said, holding up his palms in apology. "Here's what I *do* understand. Often in these situations, a missing child has been taken by someone they know, even a parent. Is it possible—"

"No," interrupted Barbara. "It definitely isn't. Jim's dad hasn't come back to Arcadia since the day he left. Not even for his belongings."

She stole another look at Merlin wearing her ex-husband's clothes and stood up to leave. Detective Scott also rose from his seat and said, "Barbara, I can see you're upset, but hang in there. I'm sure he'll turn up safe and sound."

"No offense, *Detective Scott*, but if it was Darci that went missing, do you think you'd be able to 'hang in there'?" Barbara asked, her voice trembling with restraint.

"Listen . . . officially, the department's got its hands full with the local lunatics—I mean, obviously," said Detective Scott, gesturing to the busy booking desk behind him. "But unofficially? I'll keep an eye out for your son. Promise."

Detective Scott wasn't the only one keeping an eye out for Jim. Outside the police department, Nomura lurked in her human form. Her catlike eyes narrowed as Barbara Lake barged out of the precinct, dragging Merlin into the rain behind her. The wizard tried to pull free, but Barbara tightened her grip on his beard and subjected him to another earful. They disappeared around the corner, and Nomura's painted purple lips curled into a smile— before pursing with pain.

The lithe Changeling's shoulder still troubled her after her recent run-in with Queen Usurna's goons at the museum. Nomura had been excited to return to her old "day job" and to check out the rare rock exhibit before it moved to the next stop on its tour. But instead of a polite "welcome back" reception with tea and tasteful finger foods, she was greeted by a Gumm-Gumm ambush. Narrowly escaping with her life—and a dislocated shoulder— Nomura returned to her tenuous association with Team Trollhunters and joined in their search for the missing Jim . . . not that they knew it.

Of course, she'd received Strickler's calls for assistance. But Nomura couldn't bring herself to answer them, because her pain ran far deeper than her shoulder. Changelings never admitted weakness, for to do so was to divulge an aspect of one's true identity. Yet here Nomura was, skulking in the dark and privately grieving the loss of the Troll she once loved.

Although she dedicated her entire Changeling existence to perfectly mimicking fleshbags, Nomura had never been able to re-create one central aspect of human nature: the ability to share feelings. She hissed in self-recrimination and resolved to keep her distance from the others, at least for now. So Nomura sank deeper into her isolation within the shadows, just as three other shadows passed overhead.

High above Arcadia, the Stalklings ascended with Toby and Claire clasped in their scabrous talons. Rain lashed the teens' exposed faces, and lightning streaked nearby, adding to their overall discomfort.

"On the plus side, at least this new armor kept us from getting gored by their claws!" Toby yelled over the wind. "These Stalklings could use a major pedicure!"

"Somehow, I don't think a spa day's what they had in mind, Toby!" Claire hollered back.

As the Vulture Troll tightened its hold around her body, she heard a cracking sound and hoped it came from her armor, not her ribs. Even if she still had her Shadow Staff, Claire scarcely believed she'd be able to use it. Between the Stalkling's bone-crunching grip, the rain in her eyes, and the thinning oxygen at this altitude, Claire believed she was starting to see things—things like her former history teacher flying toward them.

"Whoa! You've got wings now?!" shouted Toby, also spotting the airborne Strickler. "I still think the tweed-and-turtleneck's a better look for you, dude!"

"Let's save the fashion tips until *after* you've

graduated from sweater vests and braces, shall we, Mr. Domzalski?" Strickler said.

The Changeling tucked his wings and barreled into one of the Stalklings. Strickler pulled a feather dart from his cowl and stuck it into the Vulture Troll's back. The metal fléchette acted as a lightning rod of sorts, attracting a bolt of electricity from the heavens. The discharge turned the Stalkling to ash, but also knocked Strickler across the stratosphere.

The lightning strike also startled the other two Vulture Trolls, who accidentally released their captives. Toby and Claire cried out as they fell toward Arcadia, but their screams went unheard amidst the thunder.

CHAPTER 9
RULE NUMBER THREE

Jim and Sir Barks crept through the woods. Their alert eyes easily picked out the muddy footprints and broken branches Angor Rot had left in his wake. Jim doubted he ever would've noticed such subtleties in the past—before he got in touch with his inner Troll, that is. The trail led to a deforested clearing at the other end of the lake, where the Arcadia Oaks Dam regulated the rising river. Great torrents of water overflowed from its spillways, cascading down a steep six-hundred-foot drop. The manmade waterfall poured so powerfully, the mist obscured whatever existed over the other side of the dam.

He's around here somewhere, thought Jim. *Waiting for me to become a target out in the open, especially in a gleaming metal suit.*

Opting for a stealthier approach, the Trollhunter whispered, "For the doom of Gunmar, Eclipse is mine to command."

In a swirl of ebony energy, the Daylight Armor transformed into the Eclipse Armor. Jim mentally instructed the red piping along his body to cool, so that the armor's onyx plates better blended in to the surroundings. Sir Barks braved forward, and Jim followed like a living shadow.

Finally, thought Jim. *I've got the upper hand— not Angor Rot, for a change. And all it took was splicing my DNA with a Troll's. Go figure.*

He stepped onto the narrow cement walkway at the top of the dam, his Sword of Eclipse at the ready. Without a canopy of trees to serve as a natural umbrella, Jim felt the full weight of the downpour clatter against his armor. The Trollhunter was grateful for the chance to challenge Angor Rot to a rematch. It kept Jim in the present, distracting him from the worries gathered at the fringes of his consciousness—worries about what his mom and friends would say when they found out that Jim was . . . no longer Jim. At least, not entirely, any—

Wait, Jim thought, stopping short and signaling Sir Barks to do the same.

Peering through the veil of rain, he saw a pale gray body hunched over just ahead. It slumped there, motionless, on the dam's crest.

I must've hit Angor Rot harder than I realized! thought Jim. *But with all the mist coming off that waterfall, it's hard to tell if he's alive or dead. Probably better not to take any chances. . . .*

The Trollhunter threw the Sword of Eclipse with incredible strength and precision. The weapon pinwheeled through the air before it sank blade-first into the stationary figure's bent back. The impaled body shattered into thousands of pieces of rubble, now unquestionably dead.

"I . . . I did it?" Jim said in disbelief. "Well, *that* was easy!"

He rushed up to pile of rocks and retrieved the Sword of Eclipse. Finally rid of the menace of Angor Rot, Jim broke into a victory dance on the dam's crest, and Sir Barks playfully hopped around him. The Trollhunter smiled in relief and was about to vanish his sword when he noticed something stuck on its tip. It was a fetish—a little totem carved out of stone, just like the ones Angor Rot used to make.

"Oh no," Jim muttered in dread. "It was a trick!"

Two bark-covered arms seized him. Jim looked back and found that he was now in the clutches of a Wood Golem, its arms as thick as tree trunks. It squeezed tighter, and Jim heard splintering sounds.

Of course, Jim thought as he struggled. *Angor Rot made a Stone Golem as a decoy to lure me out, then blocked off my only other way out. Way to fall for the oldest trap in the book, Lake!*

Sir Barks bit down on one of the creature's branches and refused to let go like in a deadly game of fetch. The Golem tried to shake off the puppy, giving Jim the opportunity he needed to conjure the Glaives back into his hands. He dug them into the Wood Golem's sides, and it released Jim with a moan of pain.

"Time to whittle you down to size," said Jim, snapping the Glaives together.

He hurled the knife-edged boomerang at the Golem's knotty head and then chopped at its knees with his sword. Like a lumberjack with a grudge, Jim hacked off its legs, causing the wooden automaton to teeter and tip over.

"Timber!" yelled Jim as the Wood Golem fell over.

The Trollhunter then plunged the Sword of Eclipse into its torso, destroying the totem that had brought it to life. Adding a final insult to the injury, Sir Barks lifted his leg and relieved himself on the fallen tree beast, to which Jim said, "Good boy."

He turned around just in time to see Angor Rot come out of hiding on one of the ladders bolted into the side of the dam. The Troll climbed the rusted rungs and tossed another fetish carved from his own living rock into a puddle. Jim and Sir Barks each took a step back as a massive Water Golem coalesced in front of them. It rolled over Jim like a gargantuan raindrop, absorbing him. Trapped inside its aqueous body, Jim thrashed and gasped out bubbles, drowning again. Sir Barks barked furiously at the Golem, until Angor Rot hurled his dagger. The wolf pup barely avoided the blade by running off the dam and back into the woods.

Retrieving his dagger, Angor Rot leaned closer to the Water Golem and patiently watched the Trollhunter run out of air inside it. After the final bubble slipped past his lips, the Eclipse Armor sublimated away. Satisfied, Angor Rot reached into the Golem and fished out Jim's Amulet.

"Just as you have stripped me of my weapons, so shall I relieve you of yours," he said.

Jim's eyes fluttered inside the Water Golem. He reached behind his back, felt the totem floating there, and snapped it with his hands. The Golem popped like a water balloon, and Jim splashed onto the cement. Groggy and weakened, Jim could only cough the fluid from his lungs as Angor Rot dragged his long fingernail across the Amulet. The Troll traced a glowing tattoo across its metal surface, similar to the one he once drew upon Jim's face. That spell had allowed Angor Rot to hijack the Sword of Daylight, and Jim now moaned at the thought of what this new hex might do.

Angor Rot then wedged his nail into the seam of the Amulet's back panel. The device blinked urgently and the tattoo flared as Angor Rot pried open the Amulet, exposing the gems concealed there—including the Triumbric Stones the Trollhunter had fought so hard to acquire.

"Nooo," Jim slurred.

Ignoring the plea, Angor Rot emptied the

gemstones into a new leather pouch and cinched it around his neck like a trophy. He then tossed the spent Amulet over the dam's crest, where it became lost in the waterfall. The assassin lifted Jim bodily and held him at eye level. With a mocking, contemptuous sneer, Angor Rot said, "Look at you. Your teeth. Your horns. Your hands. You are a Troll. I am a hunter. And as such, it is now *my* turn to subject *you* to rule number three of Trollhunting."

Angor Rot drove his knee between Jim's legs, driving out a yowl of raw, animal hurt. Jim's eyes welled with pain as Angor Rot drew back his Creeper's Sun dagger, rain and poison dripping from its point. Somehow Jim used the last of his strength to kick free of Angor Rot. And the Trollhunter followed his Amulet over the side of the dam.

CHAPTER 10
WIT'S END

"You think Merlin kept the airbags when he made this armor outta spare auto parts?" asked Toby as he dropped butt-first through another cloud.

"Let's hope we never have to find out!" Claire yelled beside him.

She thought that the sight of the ground rushing toward them would have been more upsetting—like it was when she and Jim had been in free fall over the English moors in the year 501. But Claire had assumed greater control of her powers since then, especially after fighting off Morgana's possession not long ago. True, the spiritual infection had been almost fatal. But in evicting the sorceress from her body, Claire had developed new abilities in her recuperation.

Several miles below, the Creepslayerz got a serious case of the heebie-jeebies as the abandoned Shadow Staff lifted off the alley in front of them. It snagged Toby's Warhammer in its crook, then rocketed away with breathtaking speed. Like a javelin thrown by some invisible titan, the Shadow Staff zoomed across the storming sky and landed where it belonged—in Claire's awaiting armored hand. She took the Warhammer from her staff's forked end and hurled it to Toby. He caught the crystal mallet, and his descent slowed considerably.

"Pretty crafty, Claire!" cheered Toby. "Witchcrafty, that is!"

"*Gracias*, T.P." Claire grinned back, still plunging toward the earth. "Can I offer you a shadow-jump while I'm at it?"

"Nah, I'll take the scenic route," Toby joked. "Besides, someone should probably double-back and search the unfriendly skies for Count Strick-ula."

"Suit yourself," said Claire as she opened a shadow portal in midair and fell through it.

An instant later, a second black hole opened behind Stuart Electronics. Claire dropped out of it, her purple heels clicking on the asphalt. She saw NotEnrique and

Gnome Chompsky standing in front of a dumpster . . . and Steve and Eli cowering inside it.

"A-are those sky-creepers still after you?" asked Eli.

"If they are, hiding there isn't gonna help any." Claire smirked. "Vulture Trolls have excellent eyesight and aren't above picking through garbage to get their next meal."

"We weren't hiding!" Steve denied. "We were, uh, looking for Lake in here!"

"Neep," said Chompsky, slapping his forehead at the lame excuse.

"And the Stalklings' eyesight may not be their own anymore," added a voice from above.

Everyone looked up and saw Strickler and Toby descend from the sky. The Changeling's wings were singed in places from the lightning strike, but he appeared otherwise unharmed. Now back on terra firma, Toby collapsed the Warhammer and holstered it on his armor.

"I glimpsed their mirrored eyes during my initial approach," continued Strickler. "What they see, Gunmar sees."

"And that's me cue to hightail it to Glug's tub," said NotEnrique.

But Claire blocked him with her staff and a disapproving look. Satisfied NotEnrique was staying put, she turned to the others and said, "Then we better come up with a plan. If Gunmar learns Jim's missing, he and Morgana will kick off the Eternal Night *tonight*."

"'The Eternal Night'?" Eli repeated as he climbed out of the dumpster, his zip slippers squeaking with garbage juice. "That sounds fairly unspectacular."

"The inadequate one speaks true," said Merlin.

Barbara dragged the wizard into the alley and said, "Thanks for texting the meeting point, Toby. Always so considerate."

"Anytime, Doctor L," replied Toby. "I'm just impressed I got reception that many miles above a cell tower!"

"And Elijah and Steve, thank you for helping us look for Jim," said Barbara before wrinkling her nose. "But why do you both smell like garbage?"

Eli was about to answer when Steve clamped a beefy hand over his mouth. Merlin wrung the rain out of his beard and said, "Yes, well, if we're all through dispensing pleasantries, perhaps we might turn our attention to the most pressing concern of the moment. Pray tell me, before it is too late—what's for dinner?"

"Are . . . are you kidding me, Rip Van Winkle?!" Steve griped. "Who are you? And what's with those clothes? You make Pepperjoke here look like a homecoming king!"

"Aw, thanks, Steve!" said Eli. "That means a lot coming from you!"

A high-pitched whistle silenced the crowd. They all looked at Barbara, who pulled her fingers away from her mouth and said, "Listen to me. Nobody wants Jim back more than me. *Nobody*. But as much as I hate to admit it . . . Merlin may have a point. We're all hungry. Tired. At wit's end. If we're going to have any hope of finding my son, we need to be at our best. Claire, can you take us back to—"

"WHAT THE FLIP WAS THAT?!" squealed Steve, pointing beyond Barbara.

She and the others turned, seeing a glowing streak whiz into the alley, shortly followed by two specks. They looked to Barbara like turbocharged fireflies.

"Oh no!" yelped Eli, flashing back to the worst of *many* traumatic days in high school.

"Pixies," Strickler said. "If they're on the loose, our respite may need to wait."

"'Pixies'? Those don't sound so bad," said Barbara. "What do they do—sprinkle glitter and make broomsticks float?"

"We'll explain later," Toby said through the corner of his mouth. "But right now, nobody flap your gums."

"And stuff these into your ears and nose," ordered Claire, pulling handfuls of Styrofoam peanuts from a discarded box behind Stuart Electronics.

Everyone plugged their ear canals and nostrils with the synthetic white fluff. The full swarm of Pixies descended around them. They illuminated the area like strands of living string lights, but didn't attack Team Trollhunters.

That's weird, thought Claire. *They're usually all over their potential hosts the second they spot 'em.*

She and the others then watched the Pixies drop their stolen pouch of Grave Sand into the alley. Instead of zipping around at random, they fluttered in formation over it. Then, one by one, the sprites took turns slipping down to the sack and huffing the black dust within it.

They're all over that Grave Sand like Nana's kitties are with catnip! Toby thought.

Strickler sensed there was no immediate risk, so he uncovered his mouth and said, "I'd have thought Grave Sand would've addled the Pixies. Yet they seem more focused than usual. Zen, even."

"Sounds like the medication they give hyperactive kids," added Steve. "Lotsa people think it calms 'em down, but it's actually a *stimulant* to improve concentration. Uh, I mean, so I've heard other people who are *not me* say. . . ."

"Either way, if those Pixies are out of their hive, then Angor Rot probably isn't far behind," said Claire.

"Er, we got bigger problems than ol' decay-face, sis," NotEnrique said with a gulp.

He and the others watched as the Pixies started to pulse in unison. Their wings beat in time, as if they all now operated on the same unsettling frequency. Strickler watched the alley's bricks crumble away before his very eyes, only to be replaced by a stretch of the Darklands. He cried out in horror, followed in short order by the Creepslayerz, NotEnrique, and Chompsky.

"The Pixies are so jacked up on Grave Sand, they don't need to get into our heads to mess with 'em!" Toby realized before he also crumpled with utter dread.

"It's like they've turned this entire alley into one giant nightmare!" Claire said, until she, too, finally succumbed to the terror.

CHAPTER 11
THUNDER AND PLUNDER

The Trollhunter's body washed up at a place it had been many times before: the canals of Arcadia. The storm surge had deposited Jim Lake Jr. in the concrete channels of his hometown.

His limp form tangled with other debris as an undertow pulled Jim down. His face sagged and slipped beneath the abundant currents. He sank until something snagged his torn collar.

Sir Barks-a-Lot tugged Jim's head up and out of the water. The pup's legs churned furiously as he dragged the Trollhunter over to one of the sloped retaining walls. Now clear of the deluge, Sir Barks shook the moisture from his fur and prodded the Trollhunter with his snout. The young wolf had followed Jim the entire way from the dam, never losing his scent. But now the person Sir Barks had rescued—the same person who had rescued Sir Barks hours before—lay still on the canal's inclined wall. Jim did not move, and his skin turned all the bluer.

The young wolf barked for him to wake up, but he did not. Sir Barks laid down beside Jim, about to close his sad, puppy-dog eyes, when they caught a glint in the canal. Sir Barks raised his head and spotted Jim's Amulet in the mass of downed tree limbs and junk that collected at the base of the bridge.

The puppy jumped back into the canal, retrieved the device with his teeth, and dog-paddled back to Jim. Sir Barks dropped the inert Amulet on Jim's chest, where he'd seen it worn before by the Trollhunter. The wolf then howled at the moon, as if demanding that something happen.

And it did. The Amulet suddenly sparked alive, its gears whirring, its crystal face ejecting more orbs of energy. The spheres gathered inside Jim's heart and emitted a defibrillating shock. The Trollhunter gasped alive, his eyes wide with amazement, his blood pumping again. Sir Barks jumped on top of Jim and licked his face.

"I missed you, too, Barks," Jim said weakly. "And you are one *very* good doggy!"

Propping up his bruised, waterlogged body, Jim saw the canal's water level rise even higher. He took Sir Barks under one arm and climbed up the overpass's weathered beams. From the relative safety of their perch under the bridge, Jim panted, catching his breath. He and Sir Barks heard car horns honk and wet tires squeal above them as drivers traveled through the rainstorm. Jim winced at the noise, which sounded particularly shrill to his pointed ears. He hadn't missed the sounds of civilization while he was out in nature.

Maybe that's where I belong now, thought Jim. *In the wild with other animals. . . .*

He stared at the rushing waters beneath him, picturing the faces of the friends he would likely need to leave behind. Like a daydreamer imagining shapes in the clouds, Jim saw his mom smiling back at him from the swirling surface. Claire and Toby then appeared until they, too, dissolved. Now Jim saw Blinky and AAARRRGGHH!!!'s faces in the canal and wondered if he'd ever truly see them again.

"Master Jim, is that you?" asked Blinky's watery reflection.

Jim flinched at his friend's voice. Realizing that Blinky and AAARRRGGHH!!! weren't fading away as the others had, he then said to Sir Barks, "Um, how many times did I hit my head going down that waterfall?"

"Why, it is you!" Blinky enthused from below.

Sir Barks barked at the two Trolls, and AAARRRGGHH!!! said, "Ooh, puppy!"

"Blink! AAARRRGGHH!!! You're okay!" said Jim. "Pipe down, Sir Barks-a-Lot! These guys are my friends!"

"'Sir Barks-a-Lot?' What an absurd name!" said Blinkous Galadrigal.

"Hey, if it wasn't for Sir Barks, we wouldn't even be having this conversation right now," said Jim. "By the way, how *are* we having this conversation? Where the heck are you?"

"Alas, we're still in the Quagawump Swamps," said Blinky.

"But welcoming committee not great," added AAARRRGGHH!!!

"Just so. Queen Usurna promptly ambushed

us upon our arrival, and we've been holed up in a cave to avoid her Krubera guard," Blinky continued. "But as fate would have it, this cave is also home to Plunder Pools—deep wells used by greedy Trolls to hide their treasures. Over time, the artifacts filled the pools with mystical properties of their own. Such as the ability to communicate with others via two bodies of water!"

"Everything look blurry. Too cloudy," grumbled AAARRRGGHH!!!

"Yes, I can hardly see Master Jim with all these gallons in the way," Blinky said with a squint. "Aarghaumont, if you would be so kind as adjust the reception?"

Jim watched AAARRRGGHH!!!'s finger swirl around underwater, as if turning the dial on an old-fashioned television set. But the movement only made the Trolls' projected faces ripple even more.

"No, no, that seems to have made it worse," said Blinky. "Our Trollhunter's noble countenance now appears more muddled than before!"

"That's . . . probably for the best," Jim muttered.

Detecting the shift in Jim's tone, Blinky said, "Master Jim, what's the matter? You don't seem quite yourself."

"You have no idea," answered Jim. "But don't worry about me. If you're hiding out in a cave, those Kruberas will eventually find it. You should go now."

"With all due respect, Master Jim, we'll do no such thing," Blinky said sternly. "Once, perhaps, we might have run off to save our own skins, as most Trolls would."

"Especially Blinky," joked AAARRRGGHH!!!

Blinky narrowed his six eyes at the large Troll beside him, then said, "But that was before we met you and began teaching you the ways of Trollkind. And in our time together since that fateful moment, it turns out that you have also taught *us* something."

Jim's thickened eyebrows raised as he heard Blinky speak to him across the distance. AAARRRGGHH!!! nodded along next to his friend, agreeing with every word.

"You've shown us what it means to look out for others, to put somebody else's needs ahead of one's own," said Blinky, his voice thick with emotion. "In other words, Master Jim, you've shown us what it means to be *human*. And it's a lesson we've happily taken to heart."

Jim felt the first warmth he'd known since

Ronagog and Junipra's bonfire. He wanted to say something in return to his two Troll friends, but the water became more distorted between him and his friends. Blinky and AAARRRGGHH!!! turned around and reacted to something behind them.

"Krubera!" said AAARRRGGHH!!!

"Egad! They've found us!" cried Blinky.

"Blink! AAARRRGGHH!!!" Jim shouted.

He watched helplessly as several burly Troll arms reached into view and wrestled Blinky and AAARRRGGHH!!! away from their Plunder Pool. Sir Barks yapped at the Kruberas, but the connection was lost. The canal was just a canal again.

I have to help them! Jim thought desperately.

He considered the Amulet in his palm, sensing how much lighter it felt without the gems that once filled it. Angor Rot hadn't just robbed Jim of the fruits of his many Trollhunting labors. He'd also taken the only items that might prevent the Eternal Night: the Birthstone, the Killstone, and the Eye of Gunmar, otherwise known as the Triumbric Stones. No Triumbric Stones meant no Eclipse Armor. No Eclipse Armor meant no Sword of Eclipse. No Sword of Eclipse meant no way to slay Gunmar the Gold.

Thunder rumbled overhead. So, yes, as much as Jim needed to defend his friends, he needed to find a way to defend them. His eyes returned to the canal and glimpsed a stray piece of paper float beneath the bridge. It was a brochure for the Museum of Arcadia.

And just like that, a new resolve overtook Jim. It was now time for the Trollhunter to hunt once again.

CHAPTER 12
NIGHTMARE ALLEY

Claire opened her eyes, yet all she saw was more blackness. She felt a chill, even though her purple armor, and clutched her staff, willing it to open a portal back to Arcadia.

"Help!" shouted Claire, her breath fogging in the cold, dead space. "Jim, are you out there? Can you hear me? Please, hear me! I . . . I feel like we just met—like we just found each other—not that long ago. I don't want to lose you! I don't want to be lost! Not here! Not again! Not all by myself!"

She tried and tried again, but no portal came. Her tears crystallized into ice. And Claire remained stuck in the Shadow Realm.

Toby wasn't doing that well either. In his mind, he was six years old again, visiting his parents'

graves. Nana stood behind him, drying her eyes with a lace handkerchief, while a younger version of Jim put his arm around Toby's shoulders.

"I never got to say good-bye," Toby sobbed. "Not to my parents. Not even to you, Jimbo."

Now a teenager in armor again, Toby looked to the side, but his best friend was gone, as was Nana. He searched the gloomy cemetery with his eyes and called, "Jimbo?"

Toby accidentally backed into a third tombstone and wailed when he read the name engraved upon its marble surface: James Lake Junior.

Meanwhile, the Changeling originally named Waltolemew Stricklander dropped onto one knee. Never feeling so certain about anything else in his long, deceitful life, Strickler reached into his coat pocket, pulled out a small box, and opened it. A brilliant diamond ring shone from within, and he presented it to the woman before him: Barbara.

"I know I wasn't completely honest with you when we first met, but that's changed now," Strickler proposed. "*I've* changed, Barbara. All because of you."

Rather than accept the ring, Barbara laughed. Strickler watched as her face grew long and twisted until she looked like a reptile. In the blink of an eye, Barbara Lake revealed herself as a Changeling. She laughed again at Strickler's shocked face and said, "Oh, poor, foolish Walt. You of all people should've known that everything I ever felt for you was a *lie*."

Strickler wept, heartbroken. And nearby, another Changeling cried too. NotEnrique's wide, yellow eyes streamed with tears from inside a pet carrier. On the other side of the cage, he saw his surrogate family: Ophelia and Javier Nuñez, along with their daughter, Claire, and their true son, Enrique. The little blond baby blew a raspberry at NotEnrique, and Javier asked, "Are you sure it's okay to return him to the orphanage?"

"Please!" begged NotEnrique. "Gimme a second chance! I'll show ya I'm good! I'll show ya I can deserve yer love!"

"As city councilwoman, I can rewrite the laws," said Ophelia. "Not that it matters. I mean, who's ever going to adopt *him*?"

NotEnrique curled into a ball and gave up hope. That hopelessness crept over to Gnome Chompsky. The pint-sized warrior staggered out of the smashed remains of Toby's dollhouse carrying

Sally-Go-Back's broken body in his arms. Her acrylic helmet was cracked, her articulated waist snapped in twain, exposing the empty plastic mold designed by her manufacturer. But to Chompsky, Sally wasn't just another girl who was made in Hong Kong. She was the love of his life. And she was gone forever.

Eli rifled through his bulletin board filled with grainy UFO photos, crude sketches of monsters with stone for skin, and other scraps of purported paranormal phenomena.

"Where is it?" Eli said. "Where's the one piece of evidence that links it all together?"

But he stopped searching when he heard his mother call to him from downstairs, "Eli, are you up there pretending to be important again?"

"It's not make-believe, Mother!" Eli yelled back. "It's true! It has to be. It *needs* to be! I need to be a Creepslayer!"

"Well, the newsman on the TV just said it's all fake," nagged Mrs. Pepperjack without even a trace of sympathy. "Trolls, aliens, wizards, you name it. They're all part of a giant hoax, and you're the only one who ever fell for that bunk. Oh well . . . now you can go back to always being the understudy in drama club!"

"Nooooo!" Eli screamed to the heavens.

Steve thought he heard Eli's muted scream through one of the lockers behind him. He didn't know how or why, but Steve found himself back at Arcadia Oaks High School. And across the soccer field, Steve saw a blond, powerfully built man turn his back and walk away.

"Pop?" Steve called out to the man. "Pop, where are you going?"

He raced after the faceless figure, but his father always remained just out of earshot, just out of reach. Exhausted, Steve tripped and fell onto the field, begging, "Pop, don't go! I'll do better at the next game! I'll score more points! I promise I'll make you a proud papa!"

Doctor Barbara Lake tried shaking the sobbing Steve awake, just as she'd tried with the others. But they were all too far under the Pixies' spell to even respond. Barbara ran over to Merlin, who stood calmly with his back to her in the center of the alley, and said, "Merlin, we've got to do something to help the others. I can't explain it, but you and I seem to be the only ones who're immune to the—"

She stopped when the wizard turned and gazed at her with wide, haunted eyes. He grabbed Barbara's arms and said, "You see them, don't you? Don't you?! They've occupied my nightmares since the days of Avalon!"

"What, the Pixies?" asked Barbara.

"No!" whispered Merlin before staring into the distance. *"Dolls . . ."*

"'Dolls'?" Barbara repeated. "Merlin *the Wizard* is afraid of dolls?"

"Not just any dolls!" Merlin exclaimed hoarsely. "Little porcelain girl dolls, with their chipped faces, strange eyes, and horrible little voices that repeat the word 'papa'—"

"PAPA!" Steve shrieked randomly behind Barbara.

"Always 'papa' . . . until the end of time!" Merlin finished.

"This . . . explains *a lot*," Barbara said as she released the wizard and watched him collapse on the alley floor. "But it also means you're suffering from the same mass hysteria that's affecting everyone else. And I have absolutely no idea how to stop it. . . ."

CHAPTER 13
REPEAT OFFENDER

As much as the horns made his head feel heavy and awkward, Jim couldn't deny how helpful his other new attributes had become. The extra pounds of muscle on his body allowed him to run into town in record time—all while carrying a wolf. And his larger, more clawlike hands and feet let Jim scale the walls of the Museum of Arcadia like a spider.

Jim's first impulse was to let his friends and family know he was alive, but he wasn't quite ready to face them. He didn't want to see their expressions as they processed his Trollish appearance. Besides, Jim still had a score to settle with Angor Rot before he could ever allow himself to return home. If only the Trollhunter knew how close his loved ones were at the moment—trapped in their nightmarish alley exactly one block away from the museum.

Reaching the roof, Jim and Sir Barks-a-Lot looked through a wide skylight. His long, sharp fingernails scored one of the windowpanes, carving a hole in the glass. Jim reached inside, unlocked the skylight, and swung it open. He then patted his hands on his knees, signaling Sir Barks to jump into his arms.

"Going down. Next floor—sporting goods, pet supplies, and rocks and minerals," Jim joked before he jumped them into the museum.

Jim landed like a cat and set the wolf pup down on the floor. He looked at the rock show around them. The last time he'd been there, Jim stopped a hungry Gruesome with sacks of flour, and some help from Toby, Claire, and the Creepslayerz. Of course, no patrons toured the closed exhibit at this late hour. And fortunately for Jim, there weren't any security guards in sight either.

"I've really gotta stop breaking in here," he whispered. "'Repeat offender' won't exactly look great on my college applications. If they even accept semi-Trolls at Arcadia U . . ."

Jim walked over to a large geode on display. He sniffed around its pedestal and smelled ozone. He narrowed his mutated eyes and noticed thin red lines crisscrossing around the valuable crystal. Jim took a breath and steadied his hand. He reached between the beams, careful not to trigger the high-tech alarm system.

Jim successfully extracted the crystal from the invisible web, then repeated the process with five more rocks and gems. As Sir Barks kept silent vigil, the Trollhunter arranged the various stones on one of the museum benches. Vivianite, amethyst, fire opal, wulfenite, peacock coal, and obsidian all glittered in an iridescent rainbow before Jim, and he said, "Please, Vendel, guide my hand. Wherever you are . . ."

Recalling the lessons the old, white Troll had once taught him, Jim dug his fingers into the gemstones. Vendel had always used chiseling tools, but those weren't an option on this night. Thankfully, Jim's new nails did the trick, cleaving the crystals along their facets.

You humans cut stones to unlock their beauty, Jim remembered Vendel telling him. *But Trolls cut stones to unlock their power.*

As the Trollhunter chipped at the rocks, he wondered if the same could now be said of him. In cutting away his last ties to his old life, his humanity, hadn't Jim unlocked new power inside himself—*Troll power*?

Jim finished and wiped the sweat off his horned brow. He marveled at the six carved gems twinkling back at him. Jim pulled the Amulet from his torn jeans and loaded the reshaped stones into the empty chambers in its back. Closing the device's rear compartment, he watched a full spectrum of colors wash over its surface and the incantation dial start to spin. When it stopped, the Amulet presented Jim with a new order of words.

The Trollhunter's eyes set with determination as he read, "'For the pursuit of Angor, Moonlight is mine to command.'"

Merlin's Amulet activated in Jim's hands, firing off more orbs of energy, only these burned black and white. They orbited rapidly around him like a tornado, and the winds they generated blew back Sir Barks's whiskers. The wolf pup was forced to turn his head away. But when the cyclone stopped and the exhibit hall went quiet again, Sir Barks looked back and raised his ears in surprise.

Jim stood before him in an all-new suit of Moonlight Armor. Varying shades of light and dark gray swatches camouflaged its plates, and the Amulet shone like a full moon over Jim's breast. A fanged smile spread across the Trollhunter's face. He flexed in the sleek, lightweight armor and said, "These new rocks *ROCK*!"

Sir Barks growled softly, and Jim saw flashlights sweeping across the corridor in front of them. He and his little lookout instinctively backed toward the other corridor behind them. They stopped short when they heard footsteps approach from that direction too. With their only two exits blocked by patrolling security guards, Jim took Sir Barks back into his arms, unsure of which way to go. But once he felt raindrops patter against his head, he realized they had one other option.

The skylight remained open about two stories above them. Even with his upgraded Troll strength, Jim wasn't sure he could make that kind of vertical leap.

How the heck am I supposed to get up there? thought Jim as the museum guards neared.

The Moonlight Armor suddenly shifted under

him, and Jim's boots lifted off the ground. He looked down and saw that he now stood on a pair of curved metal arcs, each one about two feet in length and painted in the same gray-on-gray pattern. They reminded Jim of the jogging stilts he'd seen cutting-edge athletes and acrobats use in extreme sports competitions.

"Those'll do," whispered a very impressed Jim.

He bent his legs and jumped, the stilts vaulting the Trollhunter and Sir Barks through the skylight— and about another ten yards beyond that. By the time the guards reached the raided exhibit, all they found was a puddle of rainwater on the floor and the crystalline crumbs that crunched under their shoes.

CHAPTER 14
FATA MORGANA

"You can do this," Doctor Barbara Lake said to herself.

As the rest of Team Trollhunters confronted their worst fears along the alley, it reminded her of the virtual reality programs her hospital used to help patients deal with anxiety. Only these waking terrors seemed much more convincing than anything experienced through a headset. They seemed almost like . . .

"Fever dreams," Barbara realized, noticing the sweat beading on everyone's faces. "They have fevers. And *those* I know how to treat. I just need to diagnose the source of the infection."

She looked at the Pixies again. Their hundred-watt bodies burned brighter every time someone cried out in fright. Occasionally, one of the Pixies would break from the rest to nip at the open pouch of Grave Sand, then speedily return to the flock.

"Okay, the Pixies are the virus," said Barbara as she recalled her medical training. "And that black sand stuff is the host medium. So, to make an *anti*virus . . ."

Barbara got down on her hands and knees and feigned illness. She tried to replicate the same symptoms the others had, groaning in torment, all while crawling closer to the Grave Sand. Barbara inched over, hoping the Pixies wouldn't notice. She wondered again why she wasn't afflicted with hallucinations, with delusions, with . . .

Fata Morgana, she thought, the words popping into her head for the first time in decades.

Barbara had first heard them when she studied painting in Rome during a college semester abroad. She may not have learned how to cook like Italians do, but Barbara somehow remembered their term for "mirage."

Making it to the Grave Sand, she waited, never taking her eyes from the pouch. As soon as another Pixie landed there to feed, Barbara cinched it shut around the unsuspecting critter.

"Gotcha!" said Barbara, feeling the Pixie bounce around inside the sack. "Now, if you like that stuff so much, why don't you eat *all* of it?"

She shook the Grave Sand pouch and saw the Pixie brighten from within its folds. Giving it a few more shakes, Barbara loosened the pull strings and peeked inside. A swollen Pixie lay at the bottom. It had eaten all the Grave Sand. Its tiny, bloated body thrummed. Its glow shifted from yellow to white-hot. Barbara grabbed the Pixie and said, "Oh, no you don't! Don't go critical just yet!"

She held on to it and climbed halfway up the alley's fire escape. Barbara reached out to the other Pixies, who were floating inches away, and said, "Not until they get their medicine too."

She shut her eyes and opened her hand. The overstuffed Pixie burst in her palm. The miniature blast triggered a chain reaction, as Barbara hoped it might. Getting hit by the shockwave, the next Pixie over quickly went supernova and blew up too. In turn, the Pixie next to that detonated, as did the one next to that, and the one next to that. Most of the Pixies exploded over Barbara's head, while the ones in the periphery dropped to the ground.

The alley changed back to its usual nighttime appearance, and Team Trollhunters abruptly snapped out of the spell that had haunted them. What was left of the Pixies rained down upon Claire, Toby, Strickler, Merlin, NotEnrique, Chompsky, and the Creepslayerz like smoldering confetti. Merlin shook the fog from his head. He noticed Barbara climbing down the fire escape and said, "You did it. But how could a mere mortal woman best a foe that I, the world's mightiest wizard, could not?"

"'Mere mortal woman'?" Claire echoed in outrage.

"Not cool, dude," Toby said to Merlin as they got to his feet. "For a guy who just woke up from a thousand-year nap, that wasn't a very woke thing to say."

"Even *I* wouldn't cross that line, beard-o," said NotEnrique.

"Neep," Chompsky concurred.

"Eh, he's just jealous," Barbara said of the wizard with a wink.

She dusted the Pixie bits off her hands and started to help the others up. After she'd assisted the Creepslayerz, Eli said to his teammate, "I had no idea Jim's mom was so . . . so . . ."

"Hardcore," Steve finished for him.

Barbara then pulled Strickler off the ground, who said, "Why, thank you, Doctor. You cured us all, even if the source of your immunity remains a mystery."

"It's no mystery at all, Walt," she explained. "I'm sure the Pixies tried to mess with my head too. Only what they didn't realize is that I'm already *living* my worst fear. Ever since the day he was born, I've worried about losing Jim. I just hope my nightmare ends soon."

That's when Gunmar's remaining Stalklings landed at each end of the alley. And Barbara knew that her nightmare was nowhere near over.

CHAPTER 15
FEARFUL SYMMETRY

Angor Rot dipped his fingers into the mud and used them to draw dark lines across his pockmarked face. The war paint made him look even more gaunt. But Angor Rot did not care. This was tradition. This was ritual. This was what the hunters of old did before they claimed their final kill.

He stared at the lake and the smoldering remains of the bonfire on the shore. He awaited the inevitable. Angor Rot chose this location for a reason, wanting to end the night's battle where it began. The symmetry of burying the Trollhunter where he had been reborn pleased him.

Snap.

His yellow eye darted to the side, scanning the woods. The sound had come from there, as Angor

Rot predicted. He touched the pouch of gemstones secured around his neck and said, "I knew you would return, my not-so-human hunter. And to tread so closely before giving yourself away! It would seem Merlin's final champion has finally mastered the element of—"

A gray-streaked figure pounced out of the woods and landed in front of him. It wasn't Jim. It was Sir Barks. Angor Rot was confused. He looked up just in time to see the Trollhunter bounding high over the trees in his Moonlight Armor.

"Surprise!" Jim yelled as his jumping stilts slammed right into Angor Rot.

The impact sent the unsuspecting Troll rolling across the mud. Jim used the momentum to backflip and land with perfect balance. Like supercharged pogo sticks, the stilts gave their wearer the ability to clear a hundred feet in a single, thrilling jump before he'd land and spring forward again. Sir Barks hadn't been so crazy about the constant up and down from the museum to the lake. But to Jim, the Moonlight Armor's means of locomotion was thrilling—almost as thrilling as watching Angor Rot struggle in the slippery mud.

"I see you've come to our final fight armed with new wonders," spat the mercenary.

He pulled four prepared fetishes from his belt and threw them into the muck between them. A quartet of Mud Golems formed quickly and waddled toward Jim and Sir Barks.

"You have *no* idea," said Jim.

Jim summoned a new weapon from his Amulet. More orbs sparked out of the ticking disc and formed into a metallic longbow. The armor then generated a quiver of streamlined arrows on Jim's back. In one fluid motion, the Trollhunter nocked an arrow in his bowstring, pulled it tight, and released. The arrow shot through the air and into a Golem, piercing its totem. The mud being made a squelching sound and shrunk into a lifeless blob.

"Impossible," said a stunned Angor Rot.

Jim harpooned the second Golem with another arrow, and it fell apart. But the third Golem closed in on Sir Barks. The little wolf barked furiously as a large, dripping foot loomed over him, about to stomp down.

"Barks!" Jim shouted.

He instinctively reached out to his furry companion,

launching a camouflaged shield. It landed on top of the pup a split second before the muddy foot did. The Golem raised its leg again to inspect the damage it had done. But Sir Barks stood tall and unharmed in his own toy set of armor. The shield had conformed to his body.

"YES!" Jim cheered before he arrowed the third Golem, crumbling it, too.

Incensed, Angor Rot signaled to the last of his sentries, commanding it to charge at the Trollhunter. It knocked the bow from Jim's hand, plastering it to the ground under a ton of mud. But rather than search for his lost weapon, Jim jumped up and performed a roundhouse kick in the air. His curved stilt slashed into the Golem's fetish, and the mud monster dissolved.

Sir Barks dug out the longbow with his paws and dutifully returned it to Jim. Angor Rot's painted face became a fearful mask. He realized he was outnumbered two-to-one. The armored wolf growled, and Jim said, "Sir Barks—go for the gronk-nuks."

Angor Rot took one look at the animal's sharp, snapping teeth and ran like crazy in the other direction. Sir Barks sprinted after him, followed by the grinning Trollhunter. Angor Rot kept checking over his shoulder while his feet stumbled on the roots and leaves.

Jim no longer needed his jumping stilts, so he retracted them. In their place, cleated treads popped out of the soles of his boots, letting Jim move quickly through the woods. Pouring on the speed, Jim laughed and said, "Oh man, if only Tobes and I had these babies for Coach Lawrence's soccer practice!"

Seeing the Trollhunter gaining on him, Angor Rot broke off a branch and hurled it like a spear. Jim ran over to—and straight up—a nearby tree to avoid the branch. His cleats sank into the bark, allowing him to climb its trunk like some woodland gargoyle. Jim watched the branch sail beneath him. He smirked at a shocked Angor Rot, who continued to flee. Jim laughed as he ran sideways along the trees while Sir Barks kept pace on the ground.

But the Trollhunter's happiness died as soon as they reached a clearing in the woods. At first Jim mistook the flickering glow there for more lightning. Only these bolts stayed in place, as did the two figures held in suspended animation behind them. Ronagog and Junipra stared back at Jim with unblinking eyes from inside a stasis trap.

"I had to do something to kill the time until you returned."

Jim and Sir Barks saw Angor Rot emerge from his hiding place in the shadows, a jagged sneer across his lips. He pointed to the stasis crystals he'd arranged in a ring around the lovesick Trolls and added, "These two made for unsatisfying sport. But I thought it wise to have a contingency on hand in the event you somehow out-hunted me. And you *almost* did."

Jim snagged another arrow from his quiver and loaded it into his bow. He pointed it at Angor Rot, only for his target to step in front of the Stasis Trap holding Ronagog and Junipra. The Troll assassin was careful to stand just far enough away that he didn't become frozen too.

"Do it!" Angor Rot hissed at Jim, rattling the pouch on his neck. "Strike me down and reclaim your Triumbric Stones! Let fly your quicksilver arrow. But know that it will pass through my body— and into these besotted fools behind me."

Jim shifted his sights to Junipra and Ronagog.

He now saw that Angor Rot had positioned himself so that the three of them stood in a straight line, one in front of the other. Sir Barks growled, and Jim tightened his hold on the bowstring.

"Slay me," demanded Angor Rot. "Slay them. And in doing so, slay the final shreds of your pathetic humanity!"

Jim had his shot. All his rain-slicked fingers had to do was let go and rid the world of Angor Rot for the last time. As the storm crashed around them, the Trollhunter took aim and released his arrow.

CHAPTER 16
PEW

"This won't end well for you," said Gunmar.

His voice echoed in eerie stereo from the two Stalklings' throats even as their mirrored eyes reflected Team Trollhunters' frightened faces. With their ravenous beaks snapping and their leathery wings scraping against the alley walls, the Vulture Trolls closed in—one from the front, one from the back.

"I see now that the Trollhunter is not amongst your number," Gunmar broadcast through the possessed beasts. "He no doubt hides like the child he is, quaking in his armor out of fear of my righteous revenge. A pity none of you shall live long enough to see me smite him and usher in the Eternal Night."

"Uh, Claire-bear? Now might be a good time to

whip up one of them shadows of yours," said Toby, avoiding a swipe from the nearest Stalkling.

"I'm trying!" said Claire, mentally urging her staff to open a portal, but nothing happened. "This thing's tied to my emotions. And they're completely fried after that stroll down Nightmare Alley!"

Gunmar's laugh came out of the Vulture Trolls, echoing off the bricks and garbage dumpsters. Barbara had heard enough. She grabbed the lid off a nearby trash can and said, "Oh, put a cork in it!"

She threw the lid like a discus, and it whacked the Stalkling in front of her right in the throat, choking off the Gumm-Gumm's hyena cackle. NotEnrique's eyes bulged in amazement, and he said, "Nice arm, Doc! Now I see where yer son gets his Glaive tossin' from!"

"Quickly—to Delancy Street!" hollered Strickler.

He led the others past the dazed Vulture Troll and into the street beyond it. The second Stalkling crawled madly after them. Now out in the open, Team Trollhunters rounded the corner onto Main Street, then ran into the park at the town square. Strickler pulled more feather arrows from his cowl, gripping them between every knuckle, and said,

"We'll make our stand here. If we go any farther, we'll be in the residential area. Gunmar would surely order his Stalklings to attack our neighbors as they slept, forcing our surrender."

"And these trees should provide good cover from those flying Creepers!" said Eli.

Merlin nodded in agreement, saying, "Once again, the bespectacled, socially awkward one speaks most astutely."

"Hey, why don't you lay off my Creep-buddy, fuzz face?!" barked Steve.

As the wizard shrugged and walked away, Eli smiled at his teammate and said, "Thanks, Steve! But that tactic was just something I read in my *Mazes & Monsters* rulebook, fourth edition."

Steve slapped Eli in the back of the helmet for being such a dork; then he heard two awful shrieks. The Stalklings swooped into the town square, dive-bombing Team Trollhunters. Everyone scattered out of the way, and the Vulture Trolls skidded to a landing on the park.

"We need to buy Claire time until she can send these things packing to the Shadow Realm," said Toby. "Who's with me?"

"Neep!" answered Chompsky, punching his fist into his open hand.

The Gnome and Toby charged at one of the Stalklings, while Strickler and Merlin took on the other. Gunmar was at the controls of their bodies like a puppet master, so the Vulture Trolls moved with his grace and skill. They lunged, bit, and slashed in coordinated attacks. They moved like a soldier who'd spent a lifetime on the fields of battle.

Chompsky narrowly avoided being eaten. He removed his hat, exposing the broken end of his horn, and jabbed it into the Stalkling's foot. As the Vulture Troll screeched in pain, Toby put his collapsed weapon inside its open mouth and extended it. The Warhammer grew to its full length, opening the Vulture Troll's jaws like a car jack. The creature squawked, unable to close its beak. Claire then snuck up behind it and thrust her Shadow Staff forward. It caught the Stalkling's narrow neck between its two tines and stapled it to the ground.

"Go, Claire!" cheered Barbara from the sidelines.

"Thanks, Doctor Lake!" Claire said. "I guess it's the least I could do until my shadowmancy comes back."

"Oh, don't be so hard on yourself. You're doing great," said Barbara. "Trust me, I didn't know how to open black holes or fight flying monsters when I was your age!"

Across the square, Merlin and Strickler corralled the other Stalkling. It hissed and swung its wings at them—until two tiny hands covered its chrome eyes from behind.

"Let's see how swift ya are without yer peepers, bird brain!" NotEnrique teased.

Strickler flicked his feather darts into the distracted Vulture Troll's hide. He then stepped aside, swept back his cloak, and said, "Merlin, if you'd care to do the honors?"

The wizard casually pulled his hand from his parachute pants pocket, pointed at the Stalkling, and said, "Pew."

NotEnrique jumped clear as a bolt of electricity flew from Merlin's fingertip. The Vulture Troll blew sky-high like it had been struck by lightning.

"Bit of overkill there, wouldn't ya say, Merly?" asked NotEnrique, waving away ashes.

"Oh, that's nothing compared to what I would've done *if* I had my Staff of Avalon," boasted the wizard.

The Creepslayerz peeked their heads out from behind a park bench. Seeing that the others had subdued the Stalklings, they stood up and put away their slingshots and stink bombs. Steve scratched the back of his head and said, "So, uh . . . we *won*?"

Before anyone could answer, the first Vulture Troll pulled its neck free of Claire's Shadow Staff. Even though the Warhammer kept its jaws pried open, the Stalkling rushed toward the Creepslayerz with its hooked claws.

"Eli! Steve! Watch out!" cried Barbara.

She ran in front of the boys and protected their bodies with her own. They all shut their eyes in fear, then heard another electric sizzle. Barbara, Steve, and Eli each cracked open an eye in time to watch the smoking Stalkling lurch to a sudden stop and keel over. They half-expected to see Merlin behind it, conjuring another lightning bolt. Instead, Detective Louis Scott stood there, his mouth hanging open in confusion, his police-issued Taser still sending currents into the monster he just zapped.

Toby hastily yanked off his helmet and tossed it behind some bushes before saying, "H-hey there, Detective Scott! So, um . . . how's Darci?"

Strickler quickly changed back to his human form. He tried to block the policeman's view of NotEnrique and Chompsky, but it was too late.

"Don't even start with that theater club stuff!" warned Detective Scott. "There's no way an amateur troupe could afford special effects like these!"

Barbara let go of Steve and Eli and said, "Louis, I owe you a giant apology for lying to you. And a giant thank-you for saving us."

"I said I'd keep an eye out," Detective Scott said as he retracted the wires back into his handheld Taser.

"But how did you know to find us here, on Main Street?" asked Strickler.

"I didn't," the detective admitted. "I was responding to a call from the museum. Security cameras show some punk in a devil mask broke in and vandalized the rock show. Told you the full moon brings out all the crazies."

Steve yelped when the smoking Stalkling in front of him started to move. He backed away from it, while Merlin pushed back his extra-large T-shirt sleeves and said, "Time to finish cooking this goose, I suppose."

"Wait!" said Claire. "Gunmar knows Jim isn't

here. And if we kill this Stalkling, he'll just make some more with his Decimaar Blade to keep us busy. And we won't be able to continue our search. If only there was a way to, I don't know, take the fight to Dark Trollmarket, put Gunmar on the defensive . . ."

Eli raised his hand to speak, like he was in class, and said, "Maybe these'll help."

With his other hand, he held out a plastic baggie containing the last surviving Pixies. They bobbed slowly inside the bag, still recovering.

"I was gonna keep them in my ant farm as evidence, in case anyone, y'know, tried to cover up Arcadia's Creeper activity," explained Eli. "But a warrior always uses all the resources at his or her disposal during times of war. At least, that's what it says in my *Mazes & Monsters* rulebook, fourth edition."

Steve whooped out loud and high-fived his teammate so hard, it stung Eli's palm. Merlin pointed at the smaller Creepslayer and said, "Ooh, I *like* this one. . . ."

"Finally!" said Steve. "The old geezer shows us some respect. That's more like—"

Before he could finish the thought, Merlin poked Steve and Eli's foreheads with his index fingers. Tiny sparks passed between the wizard's hands and the Creepslayerz skulls.

"Merlin, what're you doing?!" Barbara demanded.

"Just erasing their memories of this evening's events," said the wizard.

He removed his fingers. As Steve and Eli stared ahead in a blank-faced daze, Merlin turned toward Detective Scott and performed the same task. Toby swallowed nervously and said, "You're, uh, not planning on mind-wiping all of us, right?"

"Hardly. Though I do wish I could make myself forget some of you," Merlin answered under his breath.

The wizard clapped his hands, and Steve, Eli and the detective begin walking away from Main Street in a trance. As the rest of Team Trollhunters watched them go, Merlin said, "Go home and rest, you slayers of creeps. For you both have *much* larger roles to play . . . roles beyond your wildest imaginations . . ."

CHAPTER 17
THE HUNTER'S MOON

The Trollhunter roared as the arrow left his bow. Angor Rot smiled in smug satisfaction.

At last, thought the Troll assassin. *He's sacrificed his soul, just as I sacrificed mine. Now another has paid the ultimate price. At long last, I am not alone.*

At the last second the bolt veered off-course and planted into the ground somewhere behind Angor Rot. Jim let out a deep, shuddering sigh and lowered his bow.

"You missed on purpose!" shouted Angor Rot. "All you had to do was kill the fools behind me to end this hunt! What kind of Troll are you?!"

"I'm not a Troll. At least, not one like you," Jim said. "And I *didn't* miss."

Angor Rot saw Jim's fanged smile, then turned around. The stray arrow hadn't sunk into the mud as he'd expected. Instead, the metal shaft jutted out from one of the Stasis Trap crystals around Ronagog and Junipra, cracking it open. With its magical core now exposed, Angor Rot watched the entire Stasis Trap surge and buckle—before it exploded.

The blast sent him sprawling, while Ronagog and Junipra fell to the ground. Sir Barks lowered his head, letting the armor plating on his skull and back deflect the chunks of crystal and mud.

All around them, the rain finally stopped falling. The storm clouds that once bruised the sky had parted. And by the light of the Hunter's Moon, the Trollhunter stood triumphant over his nemesis.

"I may not look like a person anymore," Jim said to Angor Rot. "But that doesn't mean I'm not still human."

The assassin tried to push himself off the earth but could not. He was still rattled by the blast. Angor Rot reached a hand toward his midsection, and Jim wondered if the Troll had caught some crystal shrapnel in his gut during the blast.

"I . . . I almost feel sorry for you," Jim continued.

"You've tried to take everything away from me. My gems. My friends. My life."

"I succeeded in those first two endeavors, hunter, and I shall soon fulfill the last," growled Angor Rot, still struggling to rise.

"No, I don't think you will," Jim said. "I don't even think you really wanted to kill me in the first place. At least, not before you took something else from me. The same thing you lost ages ago and have regretted ever since."

Angor Rot's yellow eye glared. He clutched at his side, seething with rage. Jim watched Sir Barks wake Ronagog and Junipra with a few face licks.

"But unlike you, I'd rather die than give up my soul," said the Trollhunter.

He reached for the pouch of gemstones dangling on Angor Rot's neck, about to snatch it back—when the freed Garden Troll and River Troll tackled Jim to the ground. Sir Barks came trotting up behind them, barking excitedly, and Junipra and Ronagog both yelled, "Group hug!"

"Uh, I'm happy you guys are okay too, and I'm sorry you got caught up in this whole mess to begin with," Jim grunted under their combined weight.

"But maybe now isn't the best time for a lovefest!"

Ronagog and Junipra helped Jim back to his feet, then realized they were still holding each other's hands. Remembering their previous breakup, they grudgingly let go. Jim sighed and said, "You know what, guys? I was wrong. This *is* the best time for a lovefest. Living apart from everyone . . . well, that's no way to live at all. If you find someone who loves you—no matter what world you come from or what you look like—I say keep 'em."

Junipra and Ronagog hugged and shared a kiss. Then they went right back to shoving each other again.

"You're—*ugh!*—my—*oof!*—soulmate!" said Junipra.

"No—*hgn!*—you—*gah!*—are!" replied Ronagog.

"That . . . that doesn't even make any sense," Jim said.

He rolled his eyes and grinned despite himself. But when Sir Barks howled in alarm, Jim's blood froze. The Trollhunter spun around and saw Angor Rot running toward them, the Creeper's Sun dagger held in the hand he'd curled around his abdomen.

"If you wish to die with your soul intact, so be it!" shrieked Angor Rot.

He swung the blade at Jim, who feinted to the side, his hybrid reflexes sparing his life. Sir Barks, Ronagog, and Junipra all rushed to Jim's defense, but he said, "No! Stay back!"

"You think that by saving them, you save what's left of your humanity?" snapped Angor Rot on his dagger's return swing. "That part of you is gone forever, hunter! Now there's enough Troll in you for me to turn to stone! Like I did to AAARRRGGHH!!! To Draal! Like you did to me!"

Jim blocked another of Angor Rot's stabs and kicked him away. The Moonlight Armor's cleats scraped his brittle body, yet he was too bloodthirsty to notice. Angor Rot lunged again. This time the Trollhunter was ready for him.

He purposefully fell onto his armored back and held up his legs. As the deranged Troll jumped on him, Jim replaced the treads on his boots with the jumping stilts and said, "You did that to yourself."

Angor Rot realized too late what the Trollhunter had done. He collided with Jim's stilts—and bounced right off them. As the assassin ricocheted into a tree, Jim somersaulted forward and fired another arrow from his bow. It knocked away the

Creeper's Sun dagger and skewered Angor Rot's hand to the tree's trunk.

The pinned Troll cried out in pain and outrage. He tried desperately to free his hand. Then another silver streak shot past his neck. Angor Rot looked to the side and saw his neck pouch now swinging from the arrow wedged into the branch beside him.

"Bad things happen to all of us, things we didn't even ask for or expect," Jim said, feeling the weight of the horns on his own head. "But every bad thing that's happened since you sold your soul to Morgana . . . well, that's all on you, Angor Rot."

The Trollhunter lowered his bow. Angor Rot looked incredulously at him and said, "It is customary to put a hobbled beast out of its misery at the end of a hunt. You . . . you won't even do me that honor?"

Jim shook his head. *No.*

"Then you are the better Troll," accepted Angor Rot. "And *hunter.*"

With his free hand, he pulled a cloudy crystal sphere from his belt and crushed it. Thick smoke spread around him, blocking Jim's view. When the haze cleared, Angor Rot and his dagger were gone. The only traces of his presence that he'd left behind were a single arrow in a tree . . . and the pouch full of gems still hanging from it.

EPILOGUE
FARE THEE WELL

From the remote, misty afterlife known as the Void, two spectral figures looked through their scrying window. The portal offered a glimpse of a forested stretch of the surface world, where a River Troll and a Garden Troll wed in a private ceremony. Ronagog and Junipra beamed with happiness as they exchanged nose rings—which had been fashioned from one of the Moonlight arrows—and inserted them into each other's snouts.

"Is that how you married Mother?" asked Draal's spirit in the Void.

The ghost of Kanjigar the Courageous grinned and said, "Ours was a more traditional affair. Ballustra and I first engaged in a trial-by-combat cage match before reciting our vows. It was the happiest day of our lives. That is, until you were born, my son. Why, I can still remember how we used to carry you, feed you, and wipe your little blue—"

"Ugh, Father!" Draal interrupted. "Don't make it weird. *Please*."

If phantoms could blush, Kanjigar would have. Instead, he and his son returned their gaze to the scrying window. There they saw Ronagog and Junipra wave to someone in the distance. Across the woods, Jim waved back, his and Sir Barks's camouflaged bodies practically hidden in the trees. The Trollhunter and his hound then turned and disappeared into the wild.

"Where do you think he goes now?" asked Draal. "To confront Gunmar in his new suit of armor?"

"I suspect not, my son," Kanjigar answered. "Jim Lake Junior will need his Sword of Eclipse for that final confrontation. And Dark Trollmarket has other concerns at present."

The former Trollhunter beckoned another viewing window to open. There, Draal saw the shattered, corrupted remains of the Heartstone he'd known and protected for so long in life. Gunmar the Gold stood amidst the wreckage, ordering his Gumm-Gumms into action.

"Clear this rubble at once!" barked Gunmar. "Morgana shall return from her meditations in short order, and I would have this path swept clean—so that our first steps to the Eternal Night be—"

The Gumm-Gumm king's voice faded when he saw a small black dot appear in the air before him. It rapidly widened into a vast shadow portal, and out of the vortex flew the only surviving Stalkling from the surface world. The Vulture Troll crashed into a squad of Gumm-Gumms, toppling them. Gunmar saw the blindfold tied around the Stalkling's chrome eyes before it opened its beak and vomited out a handful of Pixies.

"What trickery is this?" he shouted, seeing his soldiers drop to their knees in paroxysms of imagined terror.

Gunmar wrapped his arms around his face, covering his foul mouth, nose, and ears. But he didn't account for the last point of entry on his face—the open gouge where his right eye used to be. A Pixie darted into the socket, and the Dark Underlord felt pain sear from his horns to his hooves. He refused to feel fear. He refused to scream. He refused to acknowledge the shape that now stood at his side.

"Greetings, Father," said the apparition.

Gunmar swiveled his one good eye to look at it, and saw his own son staring back at him.

"Bular?" gasped Gunmar.

"It is I," Bular said. "For the most part."

Only now did Gunmar realize that he spoke to Bular's remains, a collection of stone fragments that were now reanimated. Bular smiled an ugly, toothsome smile at Gunmar, the rest of his incisors visible through the missing chunks of his face.

"Even in death, I have heard your shame, Father," Bular continued. "I have heard you fault me for falling at the hands of a fleshbag. But it is you who is to blame."

"Insolent whelp!" roared Gunmar. "I tolerate disrespect from none—not even my own obscene offspring!"

"But I was the best of you, as every child is of the parent that sired them," said Bular. "And if I died at the human Trollhunter's hands, then what chance does an old, half-blind Gumm-Gumm like you have against an entire *team* of them?"

Bular threw back his ruined head and laughed. And for the first time in his long, monstrous life, Gunmar finally felt fear. Gunmar finally screamed.

Back in the Void, a far different father and son closed the scrying window. Neither Kanjigar nor Draal took any satisfaction from the suffering of the Trolls who made them ghosts. Rather, they considered another portal, its surface revealing not enemies, but friends.

For Blinky and AAARRRGGHH!!! appeared in the Quagawump Swamps, their bodies bound by the Krubera guard. Queen Usurna stood imperiously before them and said, "Blinkous Galadrigal and Aarghaumont of—it saddens me to say—the Krubera. You have been declared enemies of the new Troll order. *My* Troll order!"

"Yours?" retorted Blinky. "Do you not bow before Gunmar and Morgana?"

"Hardly!" spat Usurna. "This queen bows before no others. I only bide my time and refine my strategy, manipulating those around me until my true goals are met!"

"Treat Trolls like pawns," AAARRRGGHH!!! grumbled at her.

"But of course!" Usurna boasted. "For I and I alone understand what's best for our kind, even if the rest of you are too stupid to know it!"

Blinky and AAARRRGGHH!!! noticed the Krubera around them bristle at their queen's pronouncement. Usurna dismissed her soldiers' murmuring and said, "Take that traitor to the tar pit bog. Then tie his six-eyed friend over there so he gets a good view of what comes next!"

"Bye, Blinky," said AAARRRGGHH!!! as the Trolls pulled him away.

"No, AAARRRGGHH!!!, this is not good-bye!" Blinky said back, ignoring the Kruberas fastening his body to one of the swamp's trees. "For I shall never leave the side of a friend in need! That is not the way Master Jim's humanity has shown us!"

AAARRRGGHH!!! smiled at Blinky—before a Krubera fist struck across his face. Blinky winced in sympathy as more punches and kicks came from Usurna's soldiers. The gentle giant withstood them . . . for now.

Far across time and space, Draal itched to leave the Void and fight for his friends. But Kanjigar, sensing his son's impatience, placed a translucent hand on Draal's shoulder and said, "We are forbidden to interfere, as are all Merlin's fallen champions."

"But, Father, they face certain doom in that swamp!" cried Draal.

"Do they?" asked Kanjigar. "You and I have both seen Blinkous and AAARRRGGHH!!! emerge unscathed from worse dangers than this, have we not? And even from our remove, I detect Blinky's plan already at work."

"'Plan'?" repeated Draal. "What plan?"

"Did you not see the way Usurna's soldiers reacted when she called them her pawns?" said Kanjigar. "Not all battles are fought with weapons, my son. Some are won with words. And in such wars, Blinky is the undisputed master. All he and AAARRRGGHH!!! need do is keep Usurna talking, and that queen will be the one hoisted over the tar pit bog. Nor will she be the only one to face a comeuppance of her own making. Look hither!"

Kanjigar's spirit pointed back to the scrying window, its view now shifting to the canals of Arcadia just before dawn. Angor Rot limped through the water, which had receded since the storm ended. Stifling a yell, he wrenched the Trollhunter's arrow from his hand and cast it aside with the other waste.

"Don't you know it isn't nice to litter?" murmured someone from the shadows.

Angor Rot startled when he saw two glowing cat eyes staring back at him from under the bridge. They belonged to Nomura, who stepped out of the shadows in her violet Changeling form. She pulled the scimitars from the scabbards on her back, their bent blades glinting with the last of the moonlight.

"You and I have a score to settle, assassin," said Nomura.

"You're mistaken, *Impure*," snarled Angor Rot. "Our paths have never crossed."

"No, but you crossed the path of one I once loved," she said back. "One who saw the best in me even when I did not."

Angor Rot's fingers tightened around his dagger's handle. Nomura snorted and said, "Would you even remember his face, I wonder? Out of all the lives you've taken—out of all the mayhem you've caused—which is the one that haunts you most?"

A sound came to Angor Rot, clear and unmistakable in the concrete canal. It was the single, sad coo of a dove. The rotting Troll reacted to the birdcall, but Nomura did not.

"This is a ploy!" said Angor Rot. "A bewitchment! You've turned my own Pixies against me, haven't you? Haven't you?"

Nomura pointed her scimitars at Angor Rot, and he saw two dead sprites speared upon their tips. The Changeling flicked them off her blades and said, "Your Pixies are dead. And whatever horrors you now hear aren't some bugs you can squash. They'll follow you to the end of your days like a prison—a yoke—a *leash* of your own making."

Angor Rot dropped to his knees with a splash, the dove's coo echoing louder and louder in his mind. Sheathing her swords, Nomura turned her back on the pitiful Troll, and walked away whistling *Peer Gynt*. She knew she could've assassinated the assassin right then and there. But first she wanted him to suffer the same way she had . . . ever since she lost Draal.

Little did Nomura realize that the Troll she mourned looked down upon her now from the Void. Draal's ghost stroked the window to Nomura and said, "Never change, my Changeling. . . ."

"*Now* who's making it weird?" chided Kanjigar.

Draal cleared his throat in embarrassment, then joined his smiling father. Kanjigar draped an ethereal arm on his son's back and, together, they saw a brightening horizon on one last scrying portal. As day threatened to break over Lake Arcadia Oaks, the Trollhunter and Sir Barks-a-Lot sat on its shore, taking in the last of the predawn. Jim twisted off his Amulet, dissipating his Moonlight Armor, as well as the wolf pup's. Sir Barks groaned in disappointment, making Jim chuckle while opening the device's rear hatch.

"Sorry," Jim said. "This suit definitely served its purpose, but there are only so many slots in the Amulet. And I need to load them with the only stones that have even the slimmest shot of stopping Gunmar."

He shook out the six crystals within the Amulet—the very same he'd taken "on loan" from the museum—and replaced them with the gems from Angor Rot's pouch, including the Triumbric Stones. Sir Barks looked up as Jim stood and said, "You can't come with me this time, Barks. I have a feeling something seriously bad's about to go down in Arcadia, and it's gonna take everything I've got to keep myself alive, let alone you. Besides, I think *they'd* miss you."

He nodded his horns toward the trees, where his keen Troll eyesight spotted a mother wolf and her three other pups. Sir Barks wagged his tail. He then looked from his family to Jim and back again, torn between them. Jim patted the pup's head and said, "Fare thee well, Sir Barks-a-Lot. It's been an honor to hunt alongside you. And who knows? Maybe we'll live to see each other again someday. . . ."

He watched the puppy reluctantly scamper away and be welcomed back into his pack. Sir Barks took one last look at Jim before he followed his mother and siblings back to their home in the woods.

Seeing the sun start to rise over the mountains, Jim knew he'd better get going. If he kept moving and stuck to the safety of the shadows, he figured he'd be back with his mom, Claire, Toby, and—hopefully—Blinky and AAARRRGGHH!!! plus the rest of the gang by dinnertime.

"Do you think he can do it, Father?" Draal's voice echoed from the Void. "Can he avert disaster and survive the Eternal Night?"

"It's a daunting destiny indeed that awaits him, my son," said Kanjigar the Courageous. "But if anyone can save the human and Troll worlds, then it is surely this young hero who now represents the *best* of those worlds."

Together, the father and son spirits watched Jim Lake Jr. take a deep, burdened breath. He could tell another round of changes would soon manifest through his evolving body. But Jim would just have to deal with those when they came. For the time being, though, he summoned the Eclipse Armor and made himself as ready as he could be.

The Trollhunter then took his first step toward home and the long, long night to come. . . .

READ ON FOR MORE
DREAMWORKS
TROLLHUNTERS
TALES OF ARCADIA
FROM GUILLERMO DEL TORO

Here's a sneak peek at **WAY OF THE WIZARD!**

In all his many centuries of life, Kanjigar had never known such happiness. Yes, he had felt thrilled when Rundle, son of Kilfred, father of Vendel, admitted Kanjigar into the select order of Troll scholars. And, of course, Kanjigar had been overjoyed the day he wed his bride, Ballustra. This elation only doubled later, when Kanjigar removed a chip of his own living stone, fit it against one of Ballustra's, and embedded the matching pieces in a small crystal. But even that moment paled against the swelling Kanjigar now felt in his heart.

After watching that crystal grow and glow for three decades—the average length of time for Troll development—Kanjigar and Ballustra finally heard the first, faint crack of the Birthstone. They rushed to the splintering crystal just in time to see a little blue foot kick through its opaque surface. Warm, pink light shone from within as Kanjigar broke away more shards of Birthstone and Ballustra breathed, "Husband . . . we have a son."

Kanjigar knelt before the little Troll staring back at him. Their eyes were the same. Yet Kanjigar recognized tiny versions of Ballustra's horns protruding from the newborn's head. Ballustra took their baby into her arms, nuzzled his face, and asked, "What shall we call him?"

"Draal," said Kanjigar, recalling his favorite Troll scholar.

Young Draal seemed to enjoy the name too. He smiled and gurgled while Ballustra handed him to her husband. And as a father holding his son for the first time, Kanjigar now experienced the most overwhelming sense of pride. Of peace. Of completion.

This was the greatest happiness Kanjigar had ever known.

"Look at his arms," Ballustra marveled. "He'll make a fine Monger Troll indeed!"

Kanjigar's smile faltered. He had just been

inspecting Draal's eight perfect fingers. The thought of those chubby hands holding weapons—which Monger Trolls like Ballustra made exclusively—seemed inconceivable. Kanjigar pushed the image from his mind, ignoring the imaginary war drums he had started to hear . . . only to realize they weren't quite so imaginary.

"That's a Gumm-Gumm combat march," Ballustra said, also hearing the rhythmic beat echo into their cave. "It's getting louder. Closer."

"Closer than you might think!" cried a familiar voice.

Kanjigar instinctively held Draal tighter as the Galadrigal brothers, Blinkous and Dictatious, barged into his cave, their dozen eyes bulging in terror. But when he saw the baby Troll, Blinkous clasped his four hands and added, "By Gorgus, your child is born! What a blessed occasion on such an accursed day!"

Dictatious squinted six beady eyes at Draal and said, "Is he *supposed* to look this odd?"

Ballustra moved to strike Dictatious. But Kanjigar held her back and said, "Dictatious, Blinky, you honor us as our son's first visitors. Yet what makes this day so 'accursed'? What brings those drums of war to our very threshold?"

Calming himself, Blinky said, "The Gumm-Gumms have invaded Trollmarket. Our Trollhunter, Gogun the Gentle, does his best to keep them at bay, but their numbers are legion!"

"And you've come here to *hide*?" asked Ballustra, her contempt apparent.

"No, not to hide. Only to inform Kanjigar that the Gumm-Gumms are sacking the scholars' library as we speak," Blinky said.

"But also to hide," Dictatious added hastily.

"Then it seems we've been blessed with *two more* babies on this day," said Ballustra.

She crossed to her worktable and picked up an iron crossbow loaded with crystalline arrows. As Ballustra adjusted its bowstring, Kanjigar placed a hand on her spiked shoulder.

"Wife, do not do this," said Kanjigar. "Do not go out there."

But Ballustra said, "It is my skill to make arms and my duty to take them up in battle. I am a Monger."

"You are also a mother," Kanjigar replied. "Right

now, our son needs you more than our Trollmarket. To leave our cave is to welcome death."

"Ah, but death needs no welcome," growled a darker voice. "It goes wherever it pleases."

Kanjigar felt Draal squirm in his arms, frightened by this new presence. Ballustra whirled around and aimed her weapon at the entrance to their home. Through the crossbow's sights, she saw an enormous Gumm-Gumm filling the entirety of the doorway, his hulking body threaded with veins of pale blue energy, his single eye burning bright.

"Gunmar the Black!" Blinky exclaimed.

"Begone, Gumm-Gumm," Kanjigar said bitterly. "We hold no quarrel with you."

"Yet you hold something else of interest," Gunmar snarled, black bile dripping from his jowls. "For I seek to add to our mighty ranks . . . with a recruitment drive."

Kanjigar realized with horror that Gunmar now looked directly at young Draal, as if sizing him for a miniature set of Gumm-Gumm armor. The monstrous Troll stepped deeper into the cave and said, "Enlist your whelp in my army. Or he dies on the same day he was born."

Ballustra tightened her finger around the crossbow's trigger while Kanjigar tightened his grip around their son. Gunmar moved closer, only for Blinky to defiantly block his path and say, "Now hear this, foul one! None of us will *ever* serve you! Isn't that right, brother?"

"Well . . ." Dictatious demurred from his hiding place behind Ballustra.

"You speak as though you have a choice," Gunmar said, knocking aside Blinky.

The towering Gumm-Gumm's right claw flexed, summoning pale strands of energy from his veins and molding them into the Decimaar Blade. Gunmar pointed his sword in Draal's direction and growled, "Give me your offspring—NOW. With luck, he may survive the rigors of my training and become as fine a killer as my own heir."

Kanjigar looked beyond Gunmar to see a second Gumm-Gumm darken his doorstep. This one was smaller, but his red eyes bore the same merciless glare. Still recovering on the floor, Blinky looked up and gasped, "Bular!"

Gunmar and Bular filled the cave with matching howls, making baby Draal cry. In response, Ballustra fired her arrow directly into Gunmar's chest. The Gumm-Gumm general grunted in pain, then grunted again as he yanked the crystal bolt from his hide. Bular pulled twin swords from the scabbards across his back and stalked toward Kanjigar and Draal.

Kanjigar's first thought was to shield his son from the oncoming beast. But the young Troll slipped out of his hands before he could even react. Bewildered, Kanjigar watched his son's plump face screw into an angry pout and rocky spikes pop out of his back, just like Ballustra's. Young Draal then grabbed his toes, tucked his little, naked body into a ball, and rolled headlong at Bular with incredible speed.

Caught off guard by the bizarre sight, Bular could only watch as the Troll tyke gave a tiny roar and crashed into him like a living boulder. The impact toppled Bular, sending his swords spinning in opposite directions. Kanjigar and the Galadrigals stood in stunned silence, until Blinky said, "I believe this means Draal's first word was 'RRRAAH!'"

Kanjigar reclaimed his son and looked over to Ballustra, who now fought off Gunmar's Decimaar Blade with a matching pair of battle staves. Their weapons smashed and sparked against each other, until a grating, out-of-tune horn blew in the distance.

"It's the Gumm-Gumms—they're sounding their retreat!" Dictatious said.

"Gogun must have turned the tides!" cheered Blinky.

Bular retrieved his swords, while Gunmar readied the Decimaar Blade for a final slash. But the horn blared again, far more urgently this time, followed by a stampede of hundreds of Gumm-Gumms away from Glastonbury Tor Trollmarket. Gunmar kept his one eye fixed on the family of three, even as he vanished his Decimaar Blade in a cloud of brimstone.

"You *will* serve me," Gunmar said to the infant Draal. "One day . . ."

Ballustra and Kanjigar tensed their bodies, ready for another violent attack. But Gunmar gave a low, decisive snort to Bular. The two Gumm-Gumms backed out of the cave just as quickly as they had trespassed into it.

Once the last blast of the horn faded in the distance, signaling a full withdrawal, Ballustra tossed aside the staves and took Draal back into her arms. She cradled him so close to her own body, she could feel his small heart beat against her own. Kanjigar looked at what was left of their meager belongings. He saw the broken crib and toys he'd built in anticipation of Draal's arrival, now crushed from when Bular had been bowled into them.

"You have our thanks, Kanjigar, for offering us safe haven," said Blinky. "And you, Ballustra, for defending us so vigorously."

"It's Draal who deserves your thanks, not I," said Ballustra, hoisting her boy in the air like a hero. "Not an hour out of his Birthstone and already felling grown Gumm-Gumms!"

"Hear, hear!" Dictatious called. "To Draal!"

"To Draal!" echoed Blinky.

Kanjigar was the only one to not repeat the words. For the sublime happiness he'd enjoyed upon his son's birth was now replaced by the sharp pang of a new paternal feeling—worry.

"To Draal the Deadly," said Ballustra. "The greatest warrior Trollkind shall ever know!"

RICHARD ASHLEY HAMILTON

is best known for his storytelling across DreamWorks Animation's How to Train Your Dragon franchise, having written for the Emmy-nominated *DreamWorks Dragons: Race to the Edge* on Netflix and the official Dream-Works Dragons expanded universe bible. In his heart, Richard remains a lifelong comic book fan and has written and developed numerous titles, including *Trollhunters: The Secret History of Trollkind* (with Marc Guggenheim) for Dark Horse Comics and his original series *Scoop* for Insight Editions. Richard lives in Silver Lake, California, with his wife and their two sons.